AGENT ANGEL: FIGHTING FIT

Annie Dalton

Illustrated by Lucy Truman

First published in Great Britain by
HarperCollins Children's Books 2003
This Large Print edition published by
BBC Audiobooks
by arrangement with
HarperCollins Children's Books 2007

ISBN: 978 1405 661690

British Library Cataloguing in Publication Data available

Dalton, Annie

Fighting fit /
Annie Dalton ;
illustrated by
JLP

1712056

Printed and bound in Great Britain by
Antony Rowe Ltd., Chippenham, Wiltshire

This book is dedicated to Terri, Toni and Steph, for inspiring the plot of *Fighting Fit,* to Amber, for showing me round Bath's Roman baths, and to Maria, for everything. My grateful thanks to Vivian French, Derek Levick, and Liz Nair, for suggesting such wonderful books and research materials on Ancient Rome. Any major bloopers are purely the responsibility of the author.

CHAPTER ONE

I used to think that being an angel was going to be all sweetness and light. I pictured myself zipping off to Earth, bringing peace, harmony and whatever to humankind. Then I'd zoom back to the Angel Academy, jump out of my combats, fling on a sparkly midriff top and swan off with my mates to dance till dawn. If only . . .

I adore my work, don't get me wrong. But the angel business has a definite downside. PODS are never off duty. They sabotage our missions constantly and it really gets to me sometimes.

The official term for the Powers of Darkness is the Opposition. But my mates and I just call them PODS. PODS agents are opposite to angels in every way. Unlike us they have no bodies or personalities of their own.

You think this is a drawback, right? Wrong! Over the centuries, PODS have developed the creepy ability to morph into any shape they like. But though PODS can disguise their appearance, their vibes are a dead give-away. To us anyway. Angels can suss out Dark agents immediately. So can sensitive humans; kids especially. But most people think if it looks human and acts human, it HAS to be human. They don't notice how this 'person' makes them feel.

If you're exposed to PODS toxins for any length of time, you become poisoned. Life feels like hard work. You'll go, 'Life is pointless. Why should I care what happens to this stupid planet? Turn up the TV and let someone else worry.'

See what I mean? That's not you! That's PODS talk. They want you to think life on Earth is ugly and meaningless. They want you to be depressed. When humans despair, it's MUCH harder for us to get through to you.

So far I've come back from Earth unscathed. But from time to time agents do get seriously injured. Angel trainees are especially vulnerable.

That's why our school makes Dark Studies compulsory.

I HATE Dark Study days. We're cooped up inside the Agency building for hours, while professional celestial agents put us through one simulated PODS encounter after another. These PODS set-ups are the safest way to train inexperienced angel kids and teach them to deal with the real thing. But the simulations are just SO real. By the end of the day you feel as if you've literally been dragged through the Hell dimensions and back.

After the last D.S. day, we didn't get back to our dorm until the small hours. I had a long hot shower to wash off any lingering PODS pongs (I told you simulations are realistic) and threw on my old T-shirt that says *You're no Angel.* I felt too hyper to sleep, so I went along to Lola's room to see if I could beg a mug of her special hot chocolate.

Before I could even knock, the door flew open. Lollie popped her head out. Her face was scarcely recognisable under her spooky face-pack. Without a word, she pulled me into her room, plunked a steaming mug of hot chocolate in my hand, plumped up my favourite floor cushion, so I could sit down, then calmly got on with her beauty routine.

Lola Sanchez, Lollie to her friends, is the soul-mate I've been looking for since the universe began. We're so alike it's unbelievable. We both have long legs and hair that refuses to be tamed. We have almost the exact same taste in music. We even dress similarly, though being from my future, Lola is that bit whackier. She has this mad habit of giving her friends nicknames. Our big buddy, Reuben, is Sweetpea and I'm Boo. I have no idea why!

I curled up on my floor cushion, sipping my drink and moaning about my life. 'You never get any time off in this business. It takes over your ENTIRE existence.'

'That's because we're on the fast track, babe.' Lola had to mumble through stiff lips because of her face-pack.

'The fast track to what exactly?' I

4

asked her.

'The fast track to evolution, stupid.'

'I am SO sick of that word!' I complained. 'Why does everything have to keep evolving into something else? Like forests turn into coal and coal turns into diamonds. And humans turn into angels and angels turn into— whatever angels turn into. Talk about a hyperactive universe. Why can't it just chill out for a change!'

'You know what Mr Allbright says,' my mate said in her face-pack voice. ' "Don't knock evolution, it's—" '

' "—the only game in town!" ' I quoted gloomily.

Lola went into the bathroom to wash her face. 'Heavenly vibes don't just make us peachy on the outside,' she called through running water. 'They're transforming us on the inside. This school is basically a cosmic hothouse. That's why it gets so intense.'

I sighed. 'I don't feel like I'm on the fast track to anywhere, Lollie. I feel a complete fake.'

Lola is the kind of girl who says exactly what she thinks. 'OK, as a

5

human, maybe you were a bit of a ditz,' she agreed. 'But you've changed a lot, Mel Beeby.' She came out blotting her face with a towel.

'Orlando doesn't think so,' I sighed. 'We were in the same group all day and he totally ignored me.'

My friend gave me a severe look. 'How did Mr Cutie Pie sneak into this conversation? I thought we were having a serious discussion about angelic stress.'

'I'm an angel aren't I?' I sighed. 'Plus I'm seriously stressed!'

I was beyond stressed actually. I was terminally confused.

You see back on Earth, I always knew I was going to meet this special somebody. You know how the story goes, one day our eyes would meet and it'd be like DING! Now your real life can begin!!

But thanks to a hit and run joyrider my 'real life' ended dramatically the day after I turned thirteen. On the upside, all my human problems instantly became irrelevant. What I didn't reckon on, was a whole new set.

6

For example, Dating in the Afterlife is not a subject teen advice columns tend to cover.

That's why I had no idea what to do about Orlando. Even Lola admits that Orlando is the most gorgeous boy in our school. He literally looks like an angel in one of those old Italian paintings: olive skin, dark eyes and a smile so sweet it ought to be illegal.

And this is a problem? you're thinking.

Er, no! My problem is that Orlando is a genius. Lola told me from the start that all Orlando thinks about is work. 'He has NO idea of the effect he has on girls,' she warned.

I remember watching Orlando walk through the library, soon after I started at the Academy. I'm not exaggerating, every single girl turned to look at him. They were like sun-starved sunflowers yearning after the light. Like Lola said, Orlando didn't even notice!

I despise girls who whinge on about boys who don't know they exist, and I was determined I would never join Orlando's sad little groupies.

But then I got all confused. You see sometimes Orlando *did* seem to notice me. I *wasn't* imagining it, I swear. And each time it happened, my heart totally stood still. That has to be love, right?

Just thinking about it made me sigh heavily into my frothy hot chocolate. 'I just don't know where I am,' I whimpered. 'Remember the night before our guardian angel assignments? Orlando went out of his way to walk me back to the dorm. He was SO sweet! But today I might as well have been invisible.'

My friend was brushing her glossy black curls so hard, I could see sparks. 'Mel, this is driving me nuts. There's a big beautiful universe out there. And you're boringly fixated on one good-looking boy.'

'Hello! One drop-dead gorgeous boy, thank you.'

'One drop-dead, gorgeous, mysteriously unavailable boy,' Lola pointed out brutally.

I stared at her. 'I don't believe you said that! That is SO callous!'

'It's the truth! You're obsessed, girl.

Every time we have a conversation it always comes back to Mr Cutie Pie. We could be talking about cats and you'd go, "Do you think Orlando likes cats? Maybe I could give him a sweet little kitten? Perhaps he'd notice me then?"'

'You're right. I'm hopeless,' I sighed. 'Do you think I need help?'

'I think you need a boot up your sorry angel behind,' she told me. 'Come to the gym with me, Boo!! Wake up those dozy celestial cells!'

'I keep telling you, I'm not a gym kind of girl.'

'Correction,' Lola said. 'You WEREN'T a gym kind of girl. But in your new incarnation they will call you the Workout Princess!'

Since she got back from her adventure holiday last summer, my soul-mate has totally converted to the healthy life. I had to admit her fitness regime was paying off. Angels always have a special glow, but my friend looked stunningly healthy and toned.

Miaow! I thought. Exercise really does make a girl look good!

A glorious fantasy flashed through

9

my mind. A new dynamic *moi* hurrying across the campus, sunlight glinting on my hair. Suddenly Orlando catches sight of me. I have been SO blind, he thinks. This is the girl I've been waiting for. And he rushes up to me and—well I'm sure you get the picture!

'Sweating into Lycra isn't normally my idea of fun, but I suppose I could give it a try,' I sighed.

Lola was delighted. She threw her arms around me. 'You won't regret it, Boo! Today is the first day of the rest of your life!'

I felt a twinge of guilt. My motives were nowhere near as pure as she thought.

*   *   *

The workout routine was agony to begin with. Lola literally had to drag me out of bed the first few days. But after a month or so, a miracle happened. I started waking up before my alarm went off. And check this—I was actually looking forward to my morning run!

I LOVED it. Isn't that unbelievable? I truly loved that moment when Lola and I sprinted out of the door into the pearly light of early morning and jogged down to the beach. I loved running along by the water's edge, feeling tiny shells scrunch under my trainers, then looking back and seeing our two sets of footprints in the damp sand. I even loved the ache in my muscles afterwards that told me I'd worked them to the max.

Now I'd started, Lola refused to let me slack. At lunchtime we'd grab a salad from the cafeteria, then head for the gym. She even got Reuben to make us a hip hop remix of her singing *Sisters are Doing it for Themselves*. Maybe I didn't tell you, but Lola literally sings like an angel. 'We can listen to it on our headsets,' she beamed. 'It'll give us added motivation!'

We got so carried away that we started singing aloud while we were working out. All the kids in the gym started clapping and cheering. 'Look out PODS!' one boy yelled. 'The sisters are coming to get you!'

Lola decided I was ready for the advanced martial arts class she goes to with Reuben. All trainees study martial arts as part of their angel training. Like Mr Allbright told me when I first got here, 'You can't just charm your way out of a sticky cosmic situation, Melanie. There are times when you have to fight back.'

But with Reubs, martial arts is more than a module on the heavenly school curriculum. It's a way of life. Our buddy got talent-spotted back in kindergarten and he's been training at a dojo in the Ambrosia district in every spare moment ever since.

The dojo is the simplest building in the city. It's basically a roof, supported on carved wooden pillars made from some heavenly wood that smells totally sublime. Bamboo blinds keep the dojo blissfully shady. Banners of gold and crimson silk flutter in the breeze. Some have mantras painted on them in an old angelic script. One just says *Breathe.*

The dojo master stepped out of the

shadows to greet us. Reuben introduced us and we bowed respectfully to each other. Students in baggy fighting clothes were arriving in twos and threes. They bowed to the master too and silently got on with warm-up stretches.

Omigosh, I thought. I want to wear karate gear and be calm and pure just like them.

*   *   *

I started going down to the dojo twice a week after school.

Brice came along some nights. Lola said it was part of his rehabilitation programme. I was getting used to seeing my old enemy around the campus these days. I'll admit to a bad moment when I found out he and Lola had got alarmingly close, on holiday. But in a way I could understand it. Lola has a warm heart and as you know, a bad boy with a past is incredibly hard to resist. What I could NOT understand is why Reuben and Brice were such great mates.

'You do remember that he beat you up?' I asked him one night, when we were working on my sword-fighting technique.

Reuben shook his dreads out of his eyes. 'Yeah, I remember. I'm not stupid!' He assumed a defensive crouch.

My angel buddy doesn't look that tough. He's just this skinny honey-coloured kid. But studying angelic martial arts has given him this genuine inner strength.

'But don't you mind seeing Brice every day?' I asked.

Reuben looked blank. 'Why should I mind?'

'Erm, because he tried to destroy you?'

'He did what he had to do.' Reuben made a lunge with his sword and pierced me efficiently through the chest.

'Hey, I wasn't ready,' I complained.

'Try telling that to the PODS,' he grinned.

Heavenly swords have light-beams instead of blades, so Reuben and I

14

were able to slash at each other quite merrily; we just got a temporary light overdose and went dizzy. If you used the same weapon on the PODS, however, they'd dissolve into mush.

'He left scars, Reubs,' I persisted.

With a lightning move my buddy captured my sword arm. 'I got caught off-guard,' he said. 'I won't do that again in a hurry. Brice taught me a valuable lesson.'

I freed myself with a new gravity-defying jump and was impressed to find myself hovering over Reuben's head. 'Don't you worry he might, like, defect back to the Dark Powers?'

'No,' said Reuben in a firm voice. 'Now drop it, OK?'

'OK,' I agreed reluctantly.

Unlike me and Lola, Reuben is pure angel and has never lived on Earth. Human concepts like holding a grudge are completely alien to him. So far as he was concerned, Brice had turned over a new leaf and that was that.

He grinned up at me. 'Are you planning to stay up there all night?'

'I'm not sure,' I said anxiously. 'I

15

can't seem to get back down.'

Reuben gave me a mischievous smile. 'Seen Orlando lately?'

I went crashing painfully to the floor. 'You big pig!' I complained. 'That was SO mean!'

'Focus, Melanie-san,' the dojo master said sternly. 'An angel warrior must be empty like the wind. No past. No future. Only NOW.'

My conversation with Reuben reminded me that I hadn't seen Orlando for weeks. Officially he's still at school, but like I said, the boy's a brainbox and the Agency regularly sends him on solo missions.

Next day followed the new hectic pattern: running at dawn, followed by a healthy breakfast and lessons, a quick salad and gym at lunchtime, then afternoon school. I was going to have to skip the dojo that evening. Mr Allbright wanted to talk to me about my progress. I felt a familiar sinking feeling as I went into our classroom.

I was not a big success at my Earth comprehensive and I still can't quite believe my new life is for real. It's like, deep down, I'm secretly waiting for my teachers to find out I'm a fraud.

But to my relief it was all good news.

'I'm impressed,' my teacher beamed. 'If you keep this up, you could find yourself in line for a HALO award one of these days.'

'You are kidding,' I breathed.

Mr Allbright's praise made me glow all the way back across the campus. I practically danced down the path towards our dorm, singing a happy off-key version of *Sisters are Doing it for Themselves*.

Suddenly my heart gave a skip of surprise. Orlando was walking towards me. He looked incredibly glad to see me. 'I've been looking for you everywhere, Mel!' he said. 'Where've you been?'

Was I dreaming, or had my luck finally changed? Could destiny really be this kind?

I was in a total daze. I vaguely heard Orlando ask me to meet him at the library later so we could talk. And I vaguely heard myself gasp out some pathetic reply. Then I flew upstairs to

my room going, 'Omigosh! Omigosh!'
It was official! Orlando had asked me
out!!

CHAPTER TWO

I immediately flew into a major panic.
It was the most important day of my
angelic existence and what I really
needed was a style consultation with
my soul-buddy. Unfortunately, Lola
was at the dojo. But after a nail-biting
half hour, I managed to come up with
the perfect romantic look. Denim capri
pants, and a white off-the-shoulder
gypsy top embroidered with tiny pink
butterflies. I put on the sweet silver
charm bracelet Lola gave me, splashed
on my fave heavenly fragrance
(it's called Attitude) and I was ready to
go.
    I was going on my first ever date with
the most beautiful boy in our school.
OK, so the school library isn't the most
thrilling venue. But who knew where
we'd end up after that!! Don't get

ahead of yourself, Melanie, I warned myself. Take it one step at a time.

When I walked in, there was some big meeting going on. The ground floor was jam-packed with trainees. I assumed Orlando was waiting for me upstairs. I started elbowing my way through the crowd, going, 'Excuse me. Sorry, was that your foot? Erm, excuse me.'

Then I heard a familiar voice coming from the front. 'You can't believe how bad it is, until you see it for yourselves. Nero's time is basically just a PODS' playground.'

It was Orlando.

I closed my eyes as the humiliating truth sank in. Orlando had not invited me to the library for a talk. He'd invited me to A TALK at the library.

Someone tapped me on the shoulder. 'Did I miss much?' Reuben was still in his martial arts clothes. He must have rushed over from the dojo.

'I couldn't tell you. I just got here.'

'Cool outfit,' said my buddy. 'Going somewhere special?'

'Not really,' I said in a dull voice.

19

'Could you have this conversation somewhere else?' said an irritated trainee. 'Some of us are trying to listen.'

'Sorry man!' Reuben gave him an apologetic grin. 'I'm surprised to see you here, Mel,' he whispered. 'I heard they just needed guys.'

For the first time I registered that everyone in the audience was male. What was going on? We edged towards the front. Orlando was standing on a makeshift platform, looking tired but determined.

'I literally got back from Ancient Rome a few hours ago,' he was saying. 'In forty-eight hours I'll be going back, and I hope to be taking a team of volunteers with me.'

I felt a prickle of shock. Angelic missions are coordinated by the Agency. I'd never heard of agents getting their own missions together before. Orlando wasn't even a real agent, he was still only a trainee.

'I stumbled on some alarming information during my last mission,' Orlando went on. 'I passed my findings on to the Agency. They admit they're concerned, but apparently the twenty-first century is draining most of their resources.'

I felt myself cringe with shame. Just once, could it please be someone else's century giving us all this heavenly hassle?

'I'm going to level with you,' Orlando said. 'This feels very weird. Every day, trainees are told that the essence of good troubleshooting is team work. Nine times out of ten I'd agree with this. And in the past I've given some of you a hard time for trying to go it alone.'

I felt myself go red. I knew Orlando was remembering the big fight we had on my first ever time trip to Earth. I defied him and broke a major cosmic law and came close to getting myself expelled.

'But there's always that tricky one time out of ten,' Orlando was explaining earnestly. 'I believe this is one of those times.'

He looked embarrassed. 'Listen, you guys, I have absolutely no desire to be a hero. It's not my style. But the Agency's hands are tied, so I feel it's my responsibility to bridge the gap. I asked the Agency for permission to take a trainee task force back into the field. They agreed.'

'But what would we be doing exactly?' asked a nervous trainee.

'I can't go into details at this stage,' Orlando said. 'You'll just have to trust me. I promise to keep you informed on a need-to-know basis.'

I heard guys muttering, 'Fair enough.'

'Will we get basic training?' someone asked. 'I know zip about the Romans.'

'Sure you do, they're the ones who wore togas,' quipped his mate.

'That's not actually true,' I told him snootily. 'Generally only men wore togas. And that was just for formal occasions.'

I hate speaking out in public as a rule, but fashion is one topic about which I am one hundred percent confident.

Orlando smiled. 'Volunteers will undergo a forty-eight hour intensive training course. This is a ridiculously short time to train anyone for such a dangerous mission, but it's the best we can do.'

I'd totally forgiven Orlando by this time. My dearest wish had come true. He'd finally noticed me. But he didn't only like me for my looks. He respected me. Enough to want me to fight alongside him, as an angelic equal. All these months I'd worried I wasn't good enough for this amazing boy. Then out of all the girls in our school, he picks me for his personal task force!

'So do we have any volunteers?' he asked hopefully.

A forest of hands shot up, including mine and Reuben's.

Orlando looked relieved. 'That's fantastic. Thanks guys. Erm, are there any questions?'

'What should I wear?' I asked anxiously.

Some of the guys laughed, but Orlando took my inquiry seriously.

'You'll be visible throughout the mission, so obviously the Agency will provide suitable clothes.'

Reuben and I exchanged startled glances. Trainees are rarely permitted to materialise. I'd materialised three times at most since I'd started my training, and one of those was an accident.

When the meeting was over, I raced along to Lola's room and hammered on her door. She came out, wearing puffs of cotton wool between her toes and clutching a bottle of bright pink nail varnish.

'Boo, you look totally luminous!' she exclaimed. 'Who's the lucky guy?'

'Reubs and I are going to Ancient Rome,' I said breathlessly.

My mate blinked. 'A bit sudden, isn't it?'

'I know,' I beamed. 'I thought Orlando and I were going on a date but he really wanted volunteers for a dangerous mission.'

Lola's eyes went wide with sympathy. 'You must have been upset.'

'I was,' I admitted. 'Then I told myself that a warrior must be like the wind with no past or future, only now.'

My mate gave a disbelieving snort.

'You mean you looked at Orlando's eyelids and thought, "I will follow you to the end of Time!"'

I felt myself go bright red. A telepathic soul-mate is all very well but sometimes a girl needs her privacy.

'So why didn't I hear about this big meeting?' she asked.

'It was just for guys,' I explained. 'Except for me.'

'You're the only girl he asked!'

I tried to look modest. 'Apparently.'

'He must have his reasons,' she said in a doubtful voice.

My heart did a little somersault. 'I think he loves me, Lollie.'

She gave me another searching look. 'Are you sure about that, babe?'

I felt a twinge of dismay. 'What do you mean?'

'It's just that Orlando is a really advanced being.'

'You mean I'm not good enough,' I said in a huffy voice.

'That's not what I meant,' said Lola. 'Sure Orlando loves you. He also loves trees and humming birds and head-lice. That boy loves the cotton-picking

25

cosmos, Melanie. But he lives for his work!'

I told myself that Lola hadn't seen Orlando's face as he came towards me or she wouldn't have made that hurtful head-lice comparison.

'I know he does,' I agreed. 'That's what's so incredible about him!'

'But you think he sees things like you do, *carita,* and I'm not sure he does.'

'He chose me, Lola,' I said pathetically.

Lola sighed. 'Look, just don't expect too much, OK?'

'I won't,' I promised. 'I just want to help him. You should have seen him tonight at that meeting. He's SO committed. The Agency couldn't spare the agents to deal with this Roman problem, so he's getting a team together off his own bat. Can you believe that!'

'What era are you going to exactly?' she asked.

I frowned. 'Orlando said something about Nero.'

Lola looked appalled. 'No way! That's a cosmic war zone. I can't believe the Agency's letting him take trainees!'

'He warned us it could get hairy,' I said defensively. 'How come you know so much about Ancient Rome anyway?'

'Brice used to go there on business for the PODS. He said Nero was about as psycho as a human psycho can get. Half Nero's advisers weren't human, Melanie.'

Lola's warning had the opposite effect to the one she intended.

'Angels are *supposed* to go into war zones, when humans need us,' I said stubbornly. 'That's what we're for.'

I was disappointed in my friend. It was thanks to her that I'd got myself fighting fit in the first place. She should have been thrilled I was putting my new abilities to good use.

A thrilling picture flashed into my mind. Orlando and me, fighting side by side to save the Earth from an unknown cosmic catastrophe. Maybe Lola was right. Maybe I didn't know what I was getting into. But I knew one thing. This was the proudest moment of my entire angel career.

CHAPTER THREE

'You're picking this up really quickly, sweetie. Shall we just try once more to make sure?'

I nodded dumbly.

Tia whipped half a dozen bronze hairpins out of my crown of braids and my hair tumbled loose around my face. 'Try plaiting it tighter this time,' she suggested brightly. 'We're aiming for a lovely basket-weave effect.'

It was the second day of our Ancient Roman intensive and I was totally confused. Until a few hours ago, I'd been soaking up Roman survival skills alongside the male trainees. The first part of the course was mostly theory: Roman beliefs and superstitions. And curses. Cursing was HUGE back then. If someone stole your new bracelet, you didn't call the cops. You wrote a curse, calling on the gods of the underworld to punish the thief.

We were all fascinated by Roman beliefs about the Afterlife. Like, after they died, Romans would expect to be met by a strong silent ferryman called Charon. For a couple of denarii he'd row you across an underground river called the River Styx, and deliver you to your specially designated area of the Underworld. Heroes went to the Elysian Fields. Ordinary folk wound up on the Plains of Asphodel. Villains were whisked off to a Hell dimension known as Tartarus.

'But what *really* happened to Romans when they died?' I asked the instructor.

'They got what they expected, naturally,' he grinned. 'Until they'd had time to adjust to life up here and realise there was more to the Next World than they thought.'

After Beliefs and Superstitions, we had practicals. How to conduct ourselves at banquets, appropriate behaviour in Roman temples. We had to learn about the local currency for this mission. We'd be posing as humans and like other humans we'd need to pay for the facilities—the baths for instance.

29

I still couldn't believe I'd be expected to bathe in public! Apparently if I refused, people would think I was a barbarian.

'Barbarian' was about the worst insult a Roman could throw at you. They applied it to anyone who didn't think or behave the way they did. To them, a barbarian was everything that was despicable in the human race.

As an angel, I would never diss another person's culture, but the fact is Romans had some pretty barbaric attitudes themselves.

Did you know it was perfectly acceptable for a Roman dad to reject his newborn baby, especially if it was female and he'd wanted a son? I couldn't believe it when the instructor told us that. And twin infants were routinely put out of the house to die. Romans considered twins to be bad luck. This struck me as deeply strange, considering:

   1. Their capital city was founded by a pair of twin brothers, and

   2. Two of their own gods were

twin brothers—Castor and Pollux the Heavenly Twins.

Talk about a double standard!

It was a lot to take in in a short time, but, if I say so myself, I kept up with the guys pretty well. Then halfway through the second morning, a new instructor took over. His muscles bulged under his fighting clothes and he had a scar on his cheek: a souvenir from some close cosmic shave with the PODS.

'By this time you all think the Romans were insane for holding such bizarre beliefs,' he said.

Everyone looked sheepish. That's exactly what we were thinking.

'What you need to understand is that Romans lived in constant terror. They weren't just scared of being overrun by barbarians. They were paranoid about their own people. Life was harsh for the majority and there was a real danger the starving masses would rise up and murder their rich masters in their beds. The rulers decided it would be wise to divert the peoples more violent tendencies into safer channels.

31

This is why they invented the Imperial Games.'

The instructor said these weren't what we would think of as games, but horrifying, bloodthirsty spectacles held in an arena, a kind of humungous circus ring. The Games were sometimes used to dispose of unwanted Roman citizens: convicted criminals, political troublemakers, or prisoners of war.

'But the most popular games featured professional fighters known as gladiators,' the instructor explained. 'A gladiator's life was brutal and short. He had probably been sold to the ludus—the gladiator school—as a slave. Or maybe he was a criminal who fought so bravely that his life was spared by the crowd. A few became real celebrities and had hordes of female fans, a bit like rock stars in other centuries.'

We all tittered but it was mostly to relieve tension. This was unbelievably dark stuff.

'You all have some experience of martial arts,' the instructor went on. 'So, if you should end up in the arena for any reason, you'll all be able to handle yourselves. Now there's not much time, so I'll only be able to teach you the most common fighting style. I want four volunteers to come down to the front.'

I eagerly jumped out of my seat. Finally some action!

'Not you, Melanie,' Orlando called. 'There's an agency stylist waiting for *you* upstairs.'

Can you believe that? The guys get to acquire gladiator skills and I'm sent to the makeover department. I felt SO humiliated.

I'd now spent six hours out of my precious forty-eight, mastering Roman hairdressing skills. And I'm sorry, I could not see the relevance. Was I supposed to zap the PODS with my hairpins? I don't think so!!

Whatever, it wasn't Tia's fault, so I did my best to follow her instructions. Finally, she was satisfied with my plaiting. After that she showed me how to mix a home-made face-pack, and helpfully suggested Roman household ingredients I could use in place of modern eye make-up and blusher.

'Now we've got to teach you to dress like a real Roman girl,' she beamed.

When she'd finished my historical makeover, Tia led me in front of a full-length mirror. I gazed at my reflection in astonishment. Over my tunic, I wore an outer garment known as a stola, which fell in soft folds to my ankles. Draped around my shoulders was a pretty light shawl. This was called a palla. A pair of leather sandals completed my Roman outfit. I put my hand to my throat.

'It needs something here.'

'Oops, I forgot to give you your bulla!' Tia held out a bizarre little charm.

I giggled. 'I can't wear that! It looks like a willie!!'

Tia explained that bullas were charms worn by freeborn Roman children to protect them from evil spirits. Girls wore them until they were married. On the day of her wedding a girl would sacrifice her bulla to the god of the crossroads, to show she was now a woman.

'Most of them were pretty rude, I'm afraid,' she admitted.

Tia let me hunt through her charm supply. Finally I found one I could have shown my nan without blushing, with a sweet little bee design.

Reuben popped his head around the door just as Tia was fastening it around my neck.

'We need you downstairs,' he said. 'Michael's here.'

'We're all done now, anyway,' Tia told him. 'I hope you enjoy your trip, Mel. If you get the chance, try that little pastry shop near the Temple of Vesta. Their walnut tarts are to die for!'

I stared at her. 'You lived in Nero's time! I had no idea!!'

'Yeah, well it's all ancient history now,' she laughed.

I raced after Reuben, skidding slightly in my sandals.

*   *   *

Michael looked up and smiled as we came into the hall and I felt a familiar prickle of awe.

I don't think I'll ever completely adjust to having a headmaster who is also an archangel. Though, unlike the other archangels, Michael genuinely has the human touch. Lola thinks it's because he has special responsibility for Planet Earth. His workload is so ridiculous we don't see him for days on end. Then suddenly there he'll be, strolling across the campus, chatting to some awed little kid. He'll be absolutely shattered: dark shadows under his eyes, a suit that looks as if he's slept in it. The guy doesn't take care of himself at all. He's even developing a bit of a podgy belly, which makes him look exactly like a big bear. But when Michael looks at you, it's like he's looking into your soul.

'As I was saying,' he went on humorously, 'hopefully, you all know a little more about Nero's Rome than you did before. But there are things we can't prepare you for, and if it's your first visit to this era, you can expect a certain amount of culture shock.'

Michael gave us the usual warnings

36

about keeping our eyes peeled for PODS. 'As you know, the Opposition constantly bombards Earth with negative thoughts and energy. Even professional celestial agents can find themselves adversely affected. Once you leave the safety of Heaven, it's easy to lose focus. So you must keep reminding each other why you are there, and what you came to do. Try to remember that no matter how it seems, you're always connected with your heavenly source. Good luck.'

That was it—we'd graduated! Tonight we'd be in the decadent world of Nero's Empire.

There was a sudden clatter as two Roman hairpins dropped to the floor. I'm not ready! I panicked. It was like those exam dreams, I used to have on Earth. That paralysing terror when you know you just haven't put in the hours. I fiddled frantically with another slipping hairpin. 'I can't even control my own hair,' I whimpered.

As I grovelled on the floor collecting hairpins, a new worry occurred to me. 'Omigosh!' I wailed. 'They forgot to tell me what I'm supposed to be called. It's bound to be some weird name and I won't be able to remember it.'

'Your name is Mella,' said a voice.

Michael crouched down beside me on the floor. He touched my little bee charm with a fingertip and I felt angelic volts shimmer through every cell.

'It's Latin for "Honey",' he told me. 'So you see, you chose the right charm quite by instinct.'

'I did?' I whispered. 'Omigosh, I did!'

Isn't that incredible? When I chose that bee design, I had NO idea my Roman name was going to be 'Honey'!!

Suddenly I didn't give a hoot about my hair. How can you fail when your charm has been personally touched by an archangel?

CHAPTER FOUR

In Departures, no-one turned a hair at our Roman costumes. It's always mad down there, even in the early hours of the morning. Agents milled around making calls. One girl was sitting in the lotus position beside her backpack, meditating while she waited. A group of trainees were playing a card game just inches away, but she was oblivious.

Our portal needed some last-minute TLC, but eventually we all squeezed inside. Al, my fave maintenance guy, closed the door with a thunk. Michael gave us a reassuring smile through the glass. This was huge for Orlando, and Michael wanted him to know he had the Agency's blessing.

The last moments before take-off always make me nervous. I wish Lollie was here, I thought. It feels weird going without her.

I think Reuben read my mind. In a husky, not entirely in-tune voice, he started to sing our private theme tune.

It goes, 'You're not alone. You're not alone.' One by one everyone joined in. Some of the more musical guys even put in harmonies. We were still singing as our time portal lit up and we blasted through the invisible barrier that divides the timeless angelic fields from the unpredictable world of human history.

En route, Orlando filled us in on a few essential details.

'We're going to Ostia, a Roman port, a few miles from the capital. I did tell you we'd be posing as slaves?' he added anxiously.

He hadn't, but by this time Orlando could have told us we were walking into a fiery furnace and we'd have followed him like lambs. That's the kind of angel he is.

Reuben patted my shoulder. 'May the gods protect you, my little honey bunny,' he whispered in Latin.

'You too, Sweetpea,' I answered fluently. Being able to understand every language going is one of the cooler perks of being an angel.

I noticed my buddy scratching

absently at the collar of his rough woollen tunic. I fingered the fine white cotton of my stola. How come I'm the only one on this mission wearing good clothes? I wondered. But there was no time to puzzle about this. Outside the portal, the colours had grown unbearably intense. We were coming in to land.

Seconds later I stepped out into a crowded Roman market place. I could smell fish and sewage and something that might be incense. Hungry white seagulls wheeled over my head screaming. Hello seagulls, I thought lovingly. Hello icky smells.

I was back on my favourite planet.

I don't know about you, but when I feel happy, I immediately have to tell someone!

'I think there's still a part of me that really misses being human,' I burbled. 'Like, here we are in a totally unknown sea port, in a totally unfamiliar century, but something inside says, "I'm home!"!!'

'Mel, shut up and move your angel butt, NOW!' Reuben ordered.

This was SO not the reaction I expected. Next minute my buddy practically threw me into a very smelly doorway. A shaven-headed guy in a tunic came striding past with a big stick, whacking anyone in his path. 'Make way, scum!' he bellowed, only in Latin obviously.

People scattered as a curtained litter carried by two male bearers came swaying into view. A warm salt breeze was blowing off the sea. Suddenly it lifted up a corner of a curtain, revealing a middle-aged Roman inside, lounging on piles of cushions. He glared at us and twitched the curtain closed.

I felt really shaky. I'd been in Nero's time for less than sixty seconds and I'd almost got my skull bashed in already! 'Thanks Reubs,' I said.

My buddy looked traumatised. 'That human saw us,' he said. 'That feels so weird.'

When you're invisible, you have time to adjust to being back in the material world. But if humans can SEE you, it's full-on right away.

I've been to a few eras now, but I've got to say, Ancient Rome was different right from the start. It wasn't any one thing that blew me away. It wasn't the towering public buildings of stone and marble, or the grimy Roman flats, where poor people lived packed like sardines. It wasn't the spicy whiffs of unfamiliar hot snacks, or even the babble of voices talking Latin and other ancient languages that had been totally forgotten by my time—it was everything. *Everything* was different. Even the sunlight on my skin. It seemed clearer, brighter. To me it felt like the world was still new. As if all its colours hadn't totally dried yet.

I love those first moments of a mission when you're still sussing out humans, wondering who you'll really get to know, and who'll be like, cosmic extras.

Take that girl sitting at a table outside a bar called *The Shower of Gold*. She's got an unusual face, I thought. She was loads paler than the olive-skinned locals I'd seen so far. That must mean she was wealthy enough to stay in the shade while slaves do her dirty work. The tiny rubies at her earlobes were another giveaway. That girl's been treated like a princess her whole life, I thought. You can just tell nothing has ever happened to her.

Tough-looking slaves stood by with cudgels, keeping a wary watch on the family's luggage. The girl was fussing over a fluffy little dog in her lap. It was so fluffy, in fact, you couldn't tell where its eyes were. 'Minerva's been stung, Pater,' the girl said to her dad. 'She whimpers when I touch her paw.'

Minerva, I thought. Now that IS weird. On a mission to Victorian times we met a fake medium who called herself Minerva. I'm not sure I'd have named that puppy after the Roman goddess of wisdom myself. Goddess of fluff maybe.

'It seems really swollen,' the girl persisted.

Her father didn't answer. He was gazing confusedly around at the buildings, as if he feared this was all a strange dream from which he might wake any moment.

44

At that moment I heard Orlando calling to us on a wavelength used only by angels. *Mel, Reuben! Get over here now!*

We hurried through the crowded forum following Orlando's vibes. Suddenly a gap appeared in the crowd and I saw the slave market.

The slaves in the slave market at Ostia were mostly barbarians, white-skinned tribes-people. They peered out fearfully through matted hair, shivering in their filthy rags.

We nervously joined Orlando and the others.

Typical Melanie, I hadn't thought how it would feel to be this close to half-naked humans who'd been cooped up in slave ships for weeks. For one thing, they didn't smell very nice, though this was hardly their fault. But it wasn't just the smell that made me feel ill. The air was thick with human fear and hatred. The kind of vibes that make it hard for an angel to breathe.

The dealer was chalking prices on crude wooden tags. He'd glance along the line of slaves, do a quick calculation, scribble a price and matter-of-factly hang it round someone's neck.

In the forum a shoe mender went on mending a broken buckle. The fishmonger roared out the price of his freshly-caught squid, and the owner of *The Shower of Gold* came out to place olives and fresh bread in front of the girl and her father.

It didn't seem to trouble them that dozens of fellow humans shivered a few metres away, with price tags round their necks. I'm not going to pretend I know how it feels to be a slave. This was my first ever glimpse of slavery. But when I looked into the eyes of these sullen, shivering men and women and children, I felt ashamed for humankind.

I was standing beside a hairy little barbarian, who was covered with tribal tattoos. His hair and beard were grey and his face was lined with age. But he was only about as tall as the average six-year-old.

'We'll get a good price for you,' the dealer said approvingly. 'You dwarves are worth big bucks. Can you juggle?'

The man shook his head. 'No juggle.'

The dealer sighed. 'Give me a break, sunshine. Even boneheaded barbarians can juggle a few oranges.'

'I am not Sunshine. I am Flammia,' the man said with dignity. 'I swallow fire.'

The slave dealer broke into a delighted grin. 'Well well, a fire-eating dwarf. Some days you just know Jupiter is on your side.'

When the dealer reached me, he looked me up and down as if I was a calf in the livestock market. He immediately registered the bulla. 'Hmmm, freeborn,' he muttered. 'Tall for a girl. Nicely turned-out. Quite pretty. Make someone a good ornatrix. Might get seven sestercii if I'm lucky.'

He scribbled a Roman numeral on a wooden tag and hung it round my neck. For the first time he noticed I wasn't shackled. He clicked his tongue with annoyance. 'Now how did that happen,' he grumbled and hurriedly found some rusty old shackles.

'Please don't,' said Orlando. 'She

won't try to escape.'

I was SO touched. It's like, even though we weren't real slaves, Orlando totally couldn't bear to see me in chains.

The man gave a derisive laugh. 'A slave's promise, now that's really worth having!'

'None of my friends are chained,' Orlando pointed out. 'We're here of our own free will.'

The dealer shook his head. 'I hate to hurt your sensitive feelings, sunshine,' he sighed, 'but I'd prefer a little bit of insurance.'

He went hurrying along the line of angel trainees, hanging inflated prices round their necks and securing them with chains. 'Don't know where you came from,' I heard him saying. 'But you've been well cared for. I'll get a fortune for you beauties.'

'This is sick,' Reuben whispered.

'Isn't it?' I said. 'What a way to run an empire!'

I was totally off the Romans by now.

'Be fair,' said a trainee, 'they've got incredible ideals.'

'Ooh, absolutely, plus they invented central heating!' I said sarcastically. 'I'm sorry, a civilisation built on human misery sucks.'

Just then someone came limping up to the dealer. He was really alarming looking. He'd lost part of one ear. He wore an eyepatch over one eye, and he had horrific scars on his legs. To judge from his limp, one of them was still giving him trouble. I decided he must be an old Roman legionary who'd received his injuries fighting the barbarians in some distant corner of the empire.

He must have been a good customer because the dealer was instantly all over him. 'Festus Brutus—good morning! How have the gods been treating you?' And he went into a spiel about this special purchase deal he could give him.

'That guy must be a lanista,' whispered Reuben.

'Very probably, but I don't know what that means,' I hissed back. It must be something they'd covered while I was perfecting my plaiting skills.

'It's Roman slang for "butcher",' Reuben explained. 'He's on the lookout for raw recruits he can train up for the arena.'

OMIGOSH! I thought. Suddenly everything made sense. That's why Orlando picked me for his task force! This butcher person was going to buy us for his ludus and turn us into gladiators. OK, so this might be a bit of a challenge, but if Orlando thought I could handle it, I was up for it, no question. Admittedly, you don't tend to hear about girl gladiators, but like Lola says, if you relied on history books for your info, you'd think girls didn't even exist in some time periods!

I shut my eyes and beamed a grateful message to my soul-mate. I owe you babe! All that fitness training you made me do, all that martial arts—it's finally coming together!

Next minute, it all fell apart.

The girl with the lapdog had left the bar to wander around the slave market. Now she was heading purposefully in my direction. Keep walking, I prayed. Pick someone else.

The girl walked right up to me, and looked intently into my face, almost as if she knew me from somewhere. I felt angelic tingles shimmer through my bones.

Don't do this, I pleaded silently. I'm sure you're a sweet human but I can't be your personal angel, OK? I'm on a v. dangerous cosmic mission.

The girl was a year or so older than me, but not nearly so tall. Up close I could see her eyes were grey and when she smiled I saw she had a dimple in her cheek. My nan would have said that was where she'd been touched by an angel. I had to admit there was something appealing about her. In another time, or another place, I'd have been delighted to get to know her. Just not here and now.

'This must be horrible for you,' she said quietly. 'I've always thought it strange that a country which thinks itself civilised, should be dependent on slave labour. My name is Aurelia Flavia, by the way.'

'You don't introduce yourself to slaves!' Her father had caught her up.

But there was no real energy to his words. It was like he was going through the motions. 'She probably doesn't even speak Latin!' he added in a tired voice.

I unfocused my eyes, willing them both to go away.

Aurelia didn't take the hint. 'We've been living in Britain for years,' she explained. 'My father thinks I've gone tribal!'

I was genuinely shocked to hear her mention my country.

Aurelia saw it. 'She understood, Pater! You can see how intelligent she is. Her soul shines out of her eyes.'

Her father sighed heavily. 'Souls,' he muttered. 'Just like your mother. She talked of souls.'

'Please, may we buy her?' Aurelia pleaded. 'You agreed I needed an ornatrix. She does her own hair beautifully.'

A distressing thought flitted into my head and once it was there, it refused to go away. He wouldn't, I thought. Orlando wouldn't do that to me. Omigosh, he *had!* Was that why I didn't need gladiator training? Was that why I got the deluxe Roman makeover treatment, while the others had to make do with hessian? I'd even got my own personal Roman name . . .

'Your hairstyle is so pretty!' Aurelia was prattling. 'My hair is impossible. Every slave I have just despairs.'

I wanted to howl with disappointment. Festus Brutus was prowling down the rows of slaves, checking us out for gladiator potential. If Aurelia kept chatting to me about hairstyles, he wouldn't think 'Feisty fighting girl', he'd think 'Personal maid',

Go with her, Melanie!

I heard Orlando's voice as clearly as if he'd spoken aloud. He didn't say that, I thought. He didn't say what I thought he said. Oh, but he did.

Aurelia needs you, Orlando told me. *It's why I brought you.*

You brought me to Rome so I could be some rich girl's hairdresser!

I was so upset, I only just stopped myself from stamping my foot.

All my foolish fantasies had

crumbled into dust. To think I'd imagined he saw me as an equal. A bimbo, that's all I was. A joke. I felt totally betrayed. I wanted to crawl into a hole and never come out. I was dangerously close to tears.

Bottle it up, I scolded myself. Swallow it down. Whatever. Don't let Orlando see you cry.

But just then the universe supplied an unexpected distraction. Our teachers are constantly telling us that the Agency works in mysterious ways. Like, one tiny thing can change the whole course of human history. Even a silly little fluffball of a pooch.

While I struggled with my feelings, Minerva suddenly noticed Reuben. My angel buddy has an affinity with all furry or feathered creatures. Birds, bees, dancing bears, universally adore him.

With a weird whimpering sound, the little dog jumped out of Aurelia's arms and went wriggling up to Reuben, holding up her injured paw.

Disregarding his chains, Reuben stooped down and began to pet her, talking so softly that no human would guess he was speaking in a very ancient language we use for communicating with birds and animals. I'm not nearly as fluent as my buddy but I got the basic gist.

'Did the wasp sting you?' he was saying. 'Do you want me to take the hurt away?'

Reuben touched her paw with a gentle finger. I saw an arrow of glowing pink light beam from his heart into Minerva. By the time Reubs straightened up, her limp had totally gone.

I don't know what Aurelia saw, but she was looking totally amazed. 'I want to buy the boy too,' she told her father. 'Minerva will need a kennel slave and he's obviously wonderful with animals.'

'I'm also wonderful with plants,' Reuben said shamelessly. 'Give me a free hand in the garden and you'll think you're living in paradise.'

My buddy never gets caught up with his emotions the way I do. He didn't give a hoot about missing out on gladiator school. Kennel boy, gardener, beggarman, thief—it was all one to him. He didn't need to be told that Aurelia needed us. Pure angels tend to go with the flow.

'Sixteen sestercii for the pair,' said the dealer promptly.

Aurelia's father opened his mouth to protest.

'It's a good price,' said Aurelia quickly.

Her father counted out coins with a dazed expression.

I gave Orlando a hurt look. 'I can't believe what you just did.'

'Melanie, I needed a way to get an agent into Aurelia's house. This was the obvious solution. I don't see why you're so upset. Being her ornatrix is not who you are. It's your cover.'

'It is?' I quavered. I SO wanted to believe him.

'I keep telling you, she needs your help.' Orlando said.

'Yeah, after all she's totally alone,' I said. 'Ooh, except for her rich daddy and a gazillion slaves. Not to mention helpful angels falling over themselves to heal her little puppy!'

The dealer was coming back with the lanista.

Orlando looked genuinely worried. 'Promise me you'll look after her?' *Please, Helix?* he added silently.

Helix is my angel name. Orlando was appealing to me as a fellow professional. So I had to say yes, didn't I?

The lanista and the slave-dealer were closing their deal. Any minute now, Orlando and I would be taken off to our different destinations.

My throat ached with misery. It wasn't meant to be like this.

'You could have explained,' I told him reproachfully. 'Did you think I was this little airhead who wouldn't understand?'

Orlando seemed shocked. 'Of course not! I told you at the start, you'd have to trust me.'

'Do you even know where they're taking you?' My voice cracked with distress.

But before he could answer, Orlando, the rest of his task force, plus Flammia and five regular-sized barbarians were all led away in chains by the lanista.

Aurelia was watching with a sympathetic expression. 'It's too soon for you to trust me, but maybe one day, you'll tell me your story.'

The stupid thing is, I'd sensed a bond with Aurelia from the start. I think Aurelia sensed it too. Maybe she wasn't as ordinary as I'd thought.

'Will you tell me your name?' she asked gently. I touched my bee charm and reminded myself that I was always connected with my heavenly power source.

'It's Mella,' I said huskily.

*   *   *

Aurelia's father hired horse-drawn wagons to transport us and their possessions back to Rome. Reuben went up front with Aurelia's dad.

As vulnerable females, Aurelia and I had to travel in the middle of the convoy. I thought these precautions were a bit extreme, but she explained that there were bandits on some stretches of the Via Roma.

It wasn't far to the capital city in miles, but in a Roman-style wagon train, the journey seemed to go on forever. But it gave Aurelia and me the opportunity to get to know each other. I tried not to tell too many lies. My mistress assumed I was a freeborn girl who'd fallen on hard times and been sold into slavery, and I just went along with it. To explain my unfamiliarity with Roman ways, I said I'd grown up in Carthage. Our instructors had mentioned this mysterious ancient country, and it had stuck in my brain. Mostly I got Aurelia to talk about herself.

Aurelia was born in Rome, but when she was a few months old, her dad had been posted overseas to administer Roman law to the bolshie Brits. Aurelia said she'd been happy, but there were very few Roman kids in her area, and she'd often felt isolated. 'This is the first time I've had a person of my own age to talk to in a long time,' she told me.

We both went back to gazing out of

the window. The scenery was gorgeous: shady cypresses, lush vineyards and peach groves. Now and then we'd glimpse a small red-roofed farm among the olive trees.

'My mother described this countryside so vividly that I feel as if I remember it myself,' Aurelia said in a wistful voice. 'My mother died when I was ten,' she explained. 'People say you'll get over it but you never do.'

'True,' I agreed. 'But it stops hurting so much.'

Aurelia's grey eyes went soft with sympathy. 'Did you lose your mother?'

I swallowed. 'And my little sister.'

The night before I died, Jade sat up in her sleep and said, 'You're my best sister in the universe.'

I said, 'I'm your only sister you nutcase.' Well, I didn't know it was our last conversation.

I hastily cast around for a different subject. 'I guess you must look like your mum. You certainly don't look like your dad.'

She smiled. 'I don't look like either of them. I'm adopted.'

'Oh, I'm sorry! I didn't know!' I said.

Luckily Aurelia didn't seem at all offended by my remark.

'Except for my older brother, Quintus, none of my parents' natural children survived more than a few hours after birth. When my mother's last baby was stillborn, she told my father she no longer wanted to live if she couldn't give him any more children. Next morning a slave found me on the doorstep. My mother thought it was a miracle and begged my father to adopt me. My father was so grateful to see her happy again that he agreed, even though I was only a girl.'

I couldn't imagine how it would feel, not knowing who your real parents were. My dad left us when I was six years old, but I knew him at least. 'So you have no idea who you really are?'

'No,' she said cheerfully. 'I'm a complete mystery.'

'Wow, that must be so weird. You could have other brothers and sisters somewhere.'

Aurelia laughed. 'When I was little, I was obsessed with the idea that I had a missing twin. I used to see her in my dreams. She looked exactly like me, but did all the naughty things that I was too scared to do! We would have these really long, complicated conversations.'

'You won't believe this but I had a twin fantasy, too,' I told her.

Aurelia smiled. 'Probably all lonely little girls have it.'

Inevitably, we got on to boys. Aurelia asked mischievously if anyone had ever wanted to marry me.

'In Carthage, we think thirteen is too young to marry,' I told her. That sounded snotty, so I said quickly, 'Has anyone asked to marry you?'

She blushed. 'Once.'

'Oooh!' I giggled. 'Was he a barbarian with tattoos!'

Aurelia took a breath. 'Gaius was Roman.' My smile faded. She said 'was'.

'He came to Londinium from Rome on the Emperor's business. We entertained him at my father's villa.' She glanced at me from under her lashes. 'He was very handsome.'

Was, I thought.

'He visited us several times after that. He hated British weather. All those low clouds. But I said mist could be romantic.' She darted me another look under her lashes. 'I really liked him. He was homesick and I'd make our cook prepare his favourite dishes.' She pulled a face, 'You can't imagine how disgusting most British cooking is. He started dropping in when my father was out. He was always very respectful,' she added hastily. 'We'd just talk and read together. One day we hired a boat and took a picnic on the river. There was white mist hanging in the willow branches. It looked like bridal veils. Gaius said, "You're right, mist is romantic." And he asked if I'd be his wife.'

The memory made Aurelia go dreamy-eyed.

I don't care how romantic it was, I thought. Gaius had no right proposing. She was just a kid. Then I remembered our instructor saying the average Roman woman wouldn't live beyond twenty-eight. Maybe Roman girls knew they didn't have much time. Maybe they had to grow up fast.

'Did you accept?' I asked.

'I had to say no. My father has not been himself since my mother died. I thought perhaps when we came back home.' Aurelia's voice shook slightly. 'And now it's too late.'

I waited.

'He died,' she explained huskily. 'Just a few hours after he returned home. My brother, Quintus, told us it was a sudden illness, but I fear—' she faltered. 'I fear he may have been poisoned. Oh, Mella, these are dangerous times.'

'I'm so sorry,' I told her. 'But who would—?'

I could see this subject was too painful for Aurelia. 'It's all in the past now,' she said quickly. 'Did I tell you I *am* to marry? Quintus has found me a suitor.'

'Oh,' I said. 'Erm, congratulations.'

Aurelia explained that she didn't exactly know Quintus. He was fourteen by the time she came along, almost adult by Roman standards. When their father got his British posting, Quintus had chosen to stay behind.

'These days he's one of Nero's most trusted senators. You will meet him, Mella. He still uses my father's house for entertaining important guests. It is supposed to be very beautiful.'

It was evening by the time the jumbled rooftops and towers of Rome came in sight. To get to the city gates, we had to drive through the necropolis. Romans were forbidden to bury their dead inside the city and a vast graveyard had grown up outside the city walls. It went on for miles. Sometimes I saw the flicker of camp fires, as a homeless person settled down to sleep among the dead. I saw my first Roman spook, flitting among the burial urns wearing a ghostly laurel wreath. Brice would want to stop and chat to him, I thought.

Brice has this bizarre empathy with ghosts. I suppose if you hang out in Hell dimensions long enough you'll talk to anyone. This led on to worrying about what was happening to Orlando and the others . . .

Some time later I felt Aurelia gently

shaking me. I couldn't believe I'd dozed off! A fine angel you are, Melanie! I scolded myself.

A slave helped me down from the wagon and I stumbled sleepily after Aurelia. Her dad was banging wearily on a bronze knocker, calling to the porter to let them in. This house hasn't got any windows, I thought in surprise. A peephole slid back and a wary eye looked out. I heard someone gasp, 'Thank Jupiter! The master's back!'

An elderly watchman let us in, beaming all over his face. 'Dorcas dreamed you'd come, master! She's been cooking all day long.'

Slaves came hurrying to welcome us, helping us off with our sandals, bringing jugs of warm scented water for us to wash off the dust, offering us honeyed wine.

I'm in a Roman house, I told myself. But I couldn't quite believe it.

We were in the atrium, a large central space with rooms leading off on all sides. There was a skylight in the roof to let in air, and light during the day, I guessed, because of the lack of windows. By night, oil lamps gave off a soft amber light, which reflected back from a gleaming marble floor. The furniture was minimal: a couple of couches, woven wicker chairs and a stone bust of the Emperor Nero. A fountain tinkled into an indoor pool, with gold sparkles in the marble basin.

The actual decor was totally alien to modern tastes. Three walls were painted blazing red. The fourth featured a large mural of a horribly realistic battle scene—noble-looking Romans in armour, versus hideous barbarians in chariots.

I noticed Aurelia's father look up hopefully every time someone came in. Finally he asked a slave if his son was expected home that night.

'Quintus Flavius is very busy,' the slave said tactfully. 'He sometimes finds it more convenient to stay at the palace.'

'Pater, let's go and see if mother's quince tree is still alive,' Aurelia pleaded. 'She talked so often of that tree.'

'You go, child,' he said in his tired

voice. 'I am going to rest.'

'Mella can come with me.' Aurelia seized my hand and pulled me into a room with couches arranged around a low round table. The mural in the dining room showed gods and goddesses feasting in flowery meadows.

On the far wall, beyond the open door, I was amazed to see waterfalls of white roses glimmering in the dark. Then I remembered that Romans put their gardens inside their houses! This one was completely enclosed by a beautiful stone walkway with doors opening into yet more rooms and apartments. Aurelia's house was the closest thing to a palace I had ever seen.

To her delight, the quince tree was still alive. It was old and bent but I could see tiny baby quinces gleaming faintly in the moonlight. I glanced up through the leaves and was thrilled to see stars. Stars inside your house, now that IS cool! Then I noticed Aurelia furtively wiping her eyes, so I tactfully slipped off to find Reuben.

Reubs and I had our supper in the

slave quarters. The food was actually not bad: a kind of Roman sausage, followed by small deep-fried pastries, dipped in honey. But Reuben isn't big on Earth food, so he sneakily fed most of his sausage to Minerva, who was now his faithful shadow. The other slaves stared at us quite openly while we were eating. But suspicious slaves were the least of my worries. For absolutely no reason, I was deeply depressed.

Reuben put his arm round me. 'You forgot your protection procedure didn't you?' he said sternly.

'Might have done,' I admitted.

'Well do it now. This house is seriously toxic.'

It was a relief to know these weren't my personal bad feelings. But where were they coming from?

'You think there are PODS, here in this house?' I asked nervously.

My buddy shook his head. 'Something isn't right. You should stay with Aurelia tonight.'

That was easy to arrange. When I told my mistress I was too scared to sleep by myself, she said I could sleep on a couch in her room.

'Won't the other slaves think it's strange?' I asked.

'Of course not,' she laughed. 'But if it worries you I'll say you're my personal bodyguard!'

As Aurelia's ornatrix, I had to unpack her clothes and put them away in the cedar-wood closets in her room. Then I carefully set out all her little perfume bottles, tweezers, brush, comb, pretty hairpins and so forth on her dressing table. Before she went to bed, I had to help her remove her jewellery and lock it in a special casket. You couldn't be too careful in Roman times, even in a house full of watchful slaves.

When I went to take off her bulla, Aurelia suddenly jerked away.

'Leave it on please, Mella. I *never* take it off.'

'I didn't know, sorry,' I said apologetically. I could tell I'd genuinely upset her. Romans are SO superstitious, I thought.

I helped Aurelia into her nightgown, then brushed her hair until it was smooth and silky.

'Your hair isn't so bad,' I told her. 'It's out of condition that's all. Perhaps we can buy some almond oil tomorrow. That's what Lola uses.'

'Is Lola your friend?' Aurelia asked.

'She's more like my spiritual twin,' I said truthfully.

My mistress looked wistful. 'So you actually found your twin, Mella?'

Oh yeah, I thought. So I did!

Two slaves came in, lugging a small couch between them. They solemnly positioned it to form a solid barrier between my mistress's bed and the door. They bowed to Aurelia and backed out, looking faintly puzzled. I heard one mutter, 'She's a bit small for a bodyguard.'

'Size is irrelevant with Carthaginians,' hissed his companion. 'All Carthaginian girls carry knives, it's a known fact.'

Aurelia was asleep minutes after we blew out the lamp.

I lay awake going over the events of the past few hours. I still had no idea why I was posing as a slave in Ancient

71

Rome. But the Agency had gone to a great deal of trouble to establish my cover. For some reason Aurelia was important to them. I decided I was honoured that Orlando trusted me to take care of her. *I won't let you down, I swear,* I told him silently.

Suddenly my mouth went dry with fear. Unsteady footsteps were coming towards our room. The door opened very softly and someone came in, stumbling in the dark. My heart gave a massive thump as I felt the intruder lean over me and peer into my face. I could smell his breath, a suffocating mixture of garlic, fish and alcohol. This isn't a burglar! I thought in a panic. This is deeply creepy!!

'Pollux!' he muttered in disgust. 'It's only her slave.'

For Aurelia's sake, I had to control my terror. I made my breathing deep and regular. I'm just a slave girl, I told myself, not even worth bothering with. I'm a tired slave girl dreaming whatever Roman slave girls dream about.

It worked. After some minutes,

whoever it was stumbled away.

I was trembling with shock. Omigosh, what was that about? I was almost positive the intruder wasn't PODS. But from the vibes, he wasn't totally human either.

There was no way I'd be able to fall asleep now. I lay clutching my bee charm in the dark, jumping out of my skin at every tiny household creak.

I remembered Aurelia saying, 'He may have been poisoned.'

'That girl needs you,' Orlando had said. And now I knew why.

CHAPTER FIVE

I felt so responsible for Aurelia's safety that two weeks later, I was still suffering from major angelic insomnia. At night, that is.

In the day, I only had to sit down in the sunshine to shell a few peas to find myself dropping off! One afternoon I actually dozed off at the baths.

Unlike other rich Romans, who took

hordes of slaves everywhere they went—one to unbuckle your sandals, one to help you into your litter, a third to run ahead clearing the rabble out of your way—Aurelia preferred a democratic approach. On our daily visits to the baths we took it in turns to guard our possessions. I'd watch them while she bathed and had her massage, then she'd do the same for me.

Apart from the constant risk of robbery, the atmosphere was really relaxing. I tucked my feet under me, leaned my head against the tiled wall and settled down happily to wait.

I was now a complete convert to Roman-style bathing. It was the most *sublime* experience. First you washed off the dust from the street, then you were slathered in scented oil and massaged v. vigorously by a trained masseuse. Then all the oil was scraped off with a cunning little gadget called a 'strigil'. After that you went through warm pools and sweltering steam rooms and icy plunge pools, until every last speck of dirt had been extracted from your pores. By the time you floated back on to the street, you were so clean you could hardly speak!

I watched dreamily as half-naked girls and women wandered to and fro between the steam rooms and the plunge pool. The humid air was full of soothing scents, jasmine, rose and sandalwood oils, perfumed creams and Roman shampoo. The sounds were soothing too. The whoosh of steam, the swoosh and bubble of water, the murmur of voices.

I felt safe in this scented female world. Safe enough to risk a teeny little snooze . . .

My eyes flew open in terror! I'd felt someone brush past. A pale blue robe was disappearing around the corner. Omigosh! I panicked. Aurelia's jewellery!! But to my huge relief, my mistress's possessions seemed undisturbed.

It was mid-afternoon by the time we went back out on to the street. After the languid atmosphere of the baths, the heat and noise outside seemed tremendous. A new temple was going up across the road and the air was thick with dust. Armies of sweating slaves in filthy rags, wrestled massive blocks of stone into place, as an overseer bellowed instructions.

While we looked around for our litter bearers, a guy tried to get us to buy a carpet. 'For such pretty ladies, very special price.'

Another guy was trying to sell us a jar of rejuvenating oil!

'Cheeky thing!' I fumed.

'Do you know where they get that stuff?' Aurelia grinned.

From the glint in her eye, I knew this was going to be gross.

'It comes from the gladiator schools,' she told me. 'The masseurs save all the dirty oil they scrape off the gladiators and sell it on.'

I stared at her, open-mouthed. 'Who in the world would buy dirty massage oil?'

'Deluded women,' she said. 'They believe gladiator sweat will keep them eternally young!'

'Euw,' I said faintly. 'Bottled gladiator sweat! That is so icky!!'

We eventually spotted our bearers

squatting by the roadside. They'd been waiting patiently in the heat for hours.

Most upper-class Romans wouldn't even register a bearer as a human being. But Aurelia was such a sweetie. 'These men look half-starved,' she said in a low voice. 'Give them a few denarii to buy food. We'll wait here.'

While we were waiting, I spotted a poster advertising the next day's Games. I was stunned to see a *girl* gladiator amongst the attractions. So girls really do fight in the arena I thought wistfully. This one was known as Star. Someone had added a drawing of her in a tiny leather skirt and boots, wielding a short curved sword. Her face was hidden behind a spooky metal mask.

'Have you heard of this girl?' I asked Aurelia. I turned to see her furtively examining a scrap of papyrus. I just had time to glimpse a childish drawing of a fish and what might have been a name and address, then she hurriedly slipped it inside her stola, looking flustered. 'Did you say something, Mella?' she said in an innocent voice.

Don't say Aurelia's got a new love interest already, I thought. She's only been in Rome a couple of weeks! How did that happen?

It turned out that my mistress knew all about the gladiator girl. She'd got the local goss from her masseuse at the baths. Star herself had only arrived in Rome a few weeks ago, but she was already becoming a bit of a celeb.

'You'd have to be a special person to be a girl gladiator,' I sighed enviously. I couldn't imagine where anyone would find that kind of courage.

'Gladiatrix are really just novelty acts,' said Aurelia. 'Like dwarves and exotic beasts. No-one takes them seriously.'

'They're taking this one seriously,' I pointed out. 'It says here she's mastered three different fighting styles.'

Aurelia shook her head. 'It doesn't matter if she masters three thousand. Romans admire gladiators in the ring, but they fear and despise them in real life. This girl will be an outcast all her days. When she dies, her body will be thrown in a pit with the corpses of criminals and suicides.'

'That's terrible!' I gasped.

'We Romans are a terrible people.' Aurelia looked upset. Her hand strayed to her bulla. 'Mella, do you believe—' she began.

At that moment we heard a polite cough. Our bearers had devoured their hard-boiled eggs and lentil porridge and were ready to take us home.

As we swayed and jolted through the city, tremendous waves of sound washed over us: chanting from the temples on the Via Sacra, and the tramp of hobnailed sandals as the Praetorian guard marched through the narrow streets, grimly maintaining Rome's precarious law and order. Occasional bursts of sexy music pierced the din, as we passed bars featuring saucy barbarian dancing girls. But behind our drawn curtains, Aurelia and I were in our own intimate little world.

'So who's coming to this big banquet again?' I asked with interest. 'Your brother, Quintus. Titus whatever his name is, the guy who wants to marry you. And who else?'

Aurelia sighed. 'A great many important Roman citizens and their wives. I won't know what to say to them.' She looked embarrassed. 'Actually I needed to talk to you about that. I'm afraid you won't be able to recline with us, Mella. Quintus has rather strong opinions about the status of slaves. If it was up to me—'

'Don't worry about it,' I told her. 'I'm not used to eating lying down. I'd probably choke and humiliate myself.'

'I may humiliate myself, too,' sighed Aurelia. 'My brother is making Dorcas prepare some very strange dishes.'

My mistress found her life in Rome as bewildering as I did. I'd only had a two-day intensive at the Agency and she'd spent most of her life as a foreigner amongst hostile British tribes.

In normal circumstances, her parents would have helped Aurelia learn the ropes. Unfortunately her mum was dead, and her dad was having some kind of breakdown. We'd see him first thing in the morning, making offerings to the household spirits at the family shrine. Then he'd disappear into his library and stay there, rustling through his scrolls, until a slave took him his evening meal. Just once I saw him in the garden, staring at his dead wife's quince tree with a haunted expression. He wants to die too, I thought, so he can be reunited with her on the Plains of Asphodel.

I think his son was also a major disappointment to him. Quintus Flavius still hadn't shown up at the house, so Aurelia's father sent a messenger to Nero's palace. Quintus eventually replied, sending his respects to his father along with a note to Aurelia, welcoming his sister to the Eternal City, hinting that her admirer was longing to meet her. But it seemed like he couldn't be bothered to drop in to say 'hi' in person.

Then out of the blue he sent instructions for a huge banquet to be prepared in their honour. At first, I thought he just wanted to welcome his father and sister home, in true lavish Roman style. Which was nice, if a bit late in the day. Then Quintus sent another message to Aurelia, saying she'd better buy herself a new dress, because he was bringing her future husband to meet her.

The whole thing made me deeply uneasy. All Aurelia knew about this Titus Lucretius guy was that he was one of Nero's closest advisers. Even her father hadn't met him, which seemed really disrespectful. I mean, officially her dad was still head of the household.

I looked up to see my mistress absently sliding her gold bangle back and forth on her wrist. Quintus must know how vulnerable Aurelia is, I thought. And he's deliberately taking advantage. If you ask me Quintus has way too much influence in this house.

I accidentally blurted my thoughts aloud. 'Wouldn't you rather meet this Lucretius guy before the banquet?' I would hate to meet my future husband, plus an unknown brother, in front of important Roman senators and whoever.

'Quintus sent word to say they'll be

at the amphitheatre tomorrow,' she said.

I gasped with surprise. 'You're actually going to the Games?'

Aurelia looked queasy. 'My brother says it's my duty as a Roman citizen. I was going to ask if you and Reuben would keep me company?'

Reuben was well in with the other house slaves by this time, and he was always telling me horrific stories of the mistreatment of slaves. Reuben and I must be the only slaves in captivity whose mistress actually ASKED them if they'd like to do something! So of course I said yes.

But I wasn't just going for Aurelia's sake. My reasons were mostly personal. On the same poster that featured the gladiatrix, there had been another name in tiny print. *Flammia the Fire-Eating Dwarf.*

If Flammia was performing, chances were the lanista's other recruits weren't far away. And that meant I'd *found* Orlando!

CHAPTER SIX

Next morning I felt incredibly jittery. Seeing humans hack each other to death is not a thing I ever hoped to have to see. Plus I wasn't at all sure my pure angel buddy would hold up under the strain.

On his first ever Earth mission, Reuben saved a dancing bear who was practically being beaten to death. This experience made him incredibly ill.

Reuben insisted I had nothing to worry about. 'I'm not saying I'll enjoy it,' he added hastily, 'but I'll handle it, same as you, Melanie.'

For space reasons, as well as decorum, he had to travel to the Games in a separate litter. This particular day, traffic was even worse than usual. There was some big ceremony going on at the Temple of Vesta. At one point our bearers had to stop to let a procession cross the Via Sacra. We weren't going anywhere, so I peeped round the curtain and watched.

All the devotees of Vesta were girls and women. They wore dazzling white stolas and wreaths of white roses in their hair, and carried small offerings for the goddess. As I watched them making their way towards the Temple of Vesta, chanting and swaying to the beat of a drum, I felt a tingle go down my spine. Vesta's temple was a genuinely sacred place, no doubt about it.

'Which goddess is Vesta again?' I asked my mistress. The Romans had so many gods and goddesses, it was hard to keep track.

Aurelia explained that Vesta was a particularly important goddess to Romans. 'She's the goddess of the hearth. Her temple is regarded as the hearth of Rome.'

'Is that where those girls tend the sacred flame?'

My mistress nodded. 'It's seen as a great honour to serve the goddess in this way. Vestal virgins are chosen when they're only nine or ten years old. They're taken to live in the Palace of the Vestals, where they undergo years of training. You sometimes see them being carried through the city. They wear white veils to show they are the brides of Rome. I used to dream about becoming one myself.'

'Can't they ever get married for real?'

'When their period of service is finished. But they rarely do.' Aurelia looked wistful. 'I used to think it would be wonderful to be a Vestal, then I found out what happens if you let the flame go out.'

'What happens?'

'You're stripped and beaten,' she said sombrely. 'The flame is supposed to be the spirit of Rome. If it goes out, Rome itself will fall.'

She suddenly made an irritated noise. 'I could walk to the amphitheatre faster than this! Can't the bearers take a shortcut!'

Aurelia seemed unusually stressed, but I assumed my soft-hearted mistress was dreading sitting through so much violence.

Our bearers dropped us off outside the amphitheatre. To our surprise,

Aurelia gave me and Reuben our tickets, little clay counters, and told us to go ahead. 'I'll find you inside,' she said firmly. Before we could follow her, she'd vanished into the crowd.

Reuben and I stared at each other.

'The little minx just gave us the slip!' he said. 'Do you think she's gone off to see this guy?'

I'd told him I thought someone had smuggled a note to Aurelia at the baths.

'You can't exactly blame her,' I said. 'She's going to be married off to some wrinkly old senator any day now.'

Reuben looked uneasy. 'I still don't think Aurelia should be meeting someone on the sly like this. She'll get into big trouble if she's found out.'

'I'm sure it's just a harmless flirtation,' I said. 'Aurelia's not the type to take silly risks.'

Reuben shook his head. 'You know her better than I do.'

Not that well, I thought wistfully. I'd genuinely believed we were friends. Well, as friendly as a mistress and her slave can be. Yet Aurelia hadn't breathed a word about this exciting new crush.

Reubs and I fought our way into the entrance of the amphitheatre. It was seething with fast-food and souvenir vendors.

'Sorry, man,' Reuben told one guy. 'Your little gladiator lamps are cool but we're really just passing through.'

'Why not just come out and tell him you're an angel?' I said.

'You think I should?' he said anxiously.

'I was joking, Sweetpea!'

We showed our tickets and a slave took us down a long corridor to the VIP enclosures. We emerged blinking into the sunlight and the noise of the amphitheatre.

I almost bolted when I saw how many people were inside. There must have been fifty-thousand Romans crammed in there, at least. A red awning had been unfurled over the arena to protect them from the sun. The fabric rippled in the breeze, sending waves of coloured light over the sand. Fast-food vendors went up and down the rows of seats. Officials with banners reeled off the names of which gladiator would be fighting who. Bookies were taking bets. It was mad.

Our seats were right at the front. A wooden barrier separated us from the arena. At opposite ends of this massive circus ring were pairs of ominous-looking gates. I found myself imagining the scene on the other side. Terrified prisoners of war, trained fighters in armour, bewildered slaves; all praying frantically to their gods to help them survive this savage 'entertainment'.

Aurelia came hurrying towards us, looking slightly pink. 'Sorry, I was going to buy us some stuffed dates, but the queues were impossible.'

Yeah, we believe you, I thought. People were craning forward, watching the gates with avid expressions. My palms went clammy. Something was going to happen. A herald in a white tunic ran into the arena blowing terrific blasts on a horn. The musicians struck up and the amphitheatre filled with military music. The gates burst open, and the crowd roared with excitement as the gladiators came marching out. They might be outcasts in the world outside, but here, in the arena, they were kings and they knew it. They looked amazing, in their swirly purple cloaks and gleaming helmets with nodding peacock plumes.

The gladiators' armour and weapons varied according to their fighting style. The crowd's favourite was the retiarius, the Fisherman. When he strode out with his giant fishing net and trident, all the girls and women screamed like fans at a concert. The two girl fighters, their faces hidden by strange bronze masks, also raised a big cheer.

The gladiators marched into the middle of the arena, then they formed a double line, standing back to back, raised their clenched fists and shouted out, 'We who are about to die, salute you!'

My hair practically stood on end. 'How can anyone be that brave?' I whispered to Reuben.

'It's the training,' he explained. 'Even in his death throes, a gladiator will try not to make a sound.'

90

'Reubs, are you sure you can cope with this?' I asked anxiously.

'I told you, I'll be OK,' he said calmly. 'Anyway we're not alone.'

I thought he was quoting his own lyrics, then I realised Reuben meant it literally. Every row of seats had at least one Earth angel in Roman costume. If I hadn't been so preoccupied, I'd have noticed the tingly cosmic vibes.

'Omigosh! There's so many!' I whispered to Reuben.

'Yeah, and we're going to need them,' he said grimly.

To my relief, the first part of the programme was quite tame: there was an elephant who wrote numbers in the sand with his trunk, with a bit of prompting from his minder, followed by a team of dwarves, who did mad acrobatics.

Flammia rode into the ring standing in a tiny chariot pulled by a Shetland pony, and brandishing a burning torch. The crowd loved this pocket-sized fire-eating barbarian. At the end of his act he rode out in a blazing chariot, like a miniature fire god, yelling with triumph.

Next they had warm-up fights between pairs of trainee gladiators. As each pair ran on, bravely waving their wooden swords, I felt a rush of hope. This one had to be Orlando. But it never was.

The crowd was getting restless. 'It's time they cut some throats around here!' yelled someone.

'Keep the action going!' someone else bellowed. 'We want real swords and real blood, not this kids' stuff!'

All around us people started to boo and hiss. It was the first time I understood why our teachers constantly go on about evolution. In my century, you'd never get fifty-thousand humans howling with excitement, purely because they wanted to see blood spouting from other people's internal organs.

A rotten apple whizzed past my ear, followed by a flying egg. Frustrated Romans were pelting the recruits with any missile that came to hand. The recruits ran off. Shortly afterwards another gate burst open. Twenty or thirty terrified men were forcibly dragged and prodded into the arena by amphitheatre officials.

I remembered that the Roman authorities regularly used the Games to dispose of unwanted troublemakers. These guys were probably all convicted criminals. They could handle themselves in a street brawl, but had absolutely no experience of this kind of fighting. They'd been given weapons but no armour or protective padding. But this was never intended to be a fair fight. The audience wanted to see blood flow. Well, now they were going to get it.

I won't go into details. No human should have to see the suffering we saw that day. Anyway, Reuben says it's always better to light one candle than to curse the dark, so I'm going to tell you about the angels instead.

When the killings began, the Earth angels totally disappeared from the stands. It felt like lights going out all around the amphitheatre. For a few chilling seconds, I saw this terrible place in all its gory blood-soaked darkness. Then all the lights came back on, only now they were inside the arena.

To some humans, love is just a word. You love your cat. You love chocolate. But to angels love means something quite different. To us, it's a power: a totally impersonal force that recreates the cosmos every single day. Think about it. Every moment love is creating brand new birds, and stars and blades of grass and amazed new humans to enjoy them.

You don't have to 'deserve' this love. It's just there for free. And no-one is allowed to die alone.

What we witnessed that day in the arena was desperate, but it was also inspiring. During their last agonised moments on Earth, dying humans were shown pure love by unknown angels. And you know what? It gave me new courage. Those angels reminded me who I really was. I wasn't really a part of this human drama. I was just an angel passing through. But that was no reason not to help.

Reuben and I had joined in with our

Roman colleagues, beaming loving vibes. For obvious reasons this took all our concentration. Then suddenly I thought to check on Aurelia. She'd gone as white as a sheet. She was clutching her bulla as if she was terrified to let it go, whispering something over and over.

But all nightmares end eventually, even this one. The mutilated bodies were dragged out of the arena. Slaves raked fresh sand over the bloodstains. But they couldn't hide the smell. It simmered in the steamy summer air like something from a Hell dimension.

I don't know what made me look behind then. It's as if I knew Orlando would be there. He was talking to the lanista, looking tired and pale. I went weak with relief. He was here, and he was OK!

Aurelia was trying to pull herself together. 'Mella, your gladiatrix is on next,' she said bravely.

Star had been paired with Juno, the only other girl fighter on the programme. Probably Star and Juno ate the same rations at the same table, slept in the same room and borrowed each other's perfume and hairpins. Now they had to try to kill each other or they wouldn't get paid.

The girls hurtled towards each other from opposite ends of the arena, swords flashing in the sun. Guys yelled obscene comments from the stands, wanting the girls to show them what they had under their leather chest bands. But they were immediately shouted down. Star and Juno were big favourites, and I soon saw why. If gladiators were kings of the arena, these girl fighters were warrior queens. And Star was just amazing.

Juno was stronger and more cunning, but Star was lighter, faster and more graceful and took crazier risks.

You know how a great dancer can make you feel as if she's dancing for you? Like she IS you, almost? That's how I felt watching Star. It was me with the sun beating on my bare neck. It was me out there on the burning sand with leather thongs tied round my bare arms and an intricately plaited hairstyle. Star was an artist. A fabulous, daring, totally lethal artist.

Aurelia was totally entranced. 'I feel as if I know her.' She put her hand to her heart. 'I know her in here.'

'I know!' I said. 'Me too.' I suddenly heard what I was saying. Melanie this is outrageous! I scolded myself. Star's a killer. You've got no business admiring her!

It was like I'd hexed the gladiatrix with my thoughts, because the very next second, Star's foot slipped from under her. Juno pounced, slashing at her with her sword. Star faltered, then renewed her furious attack. She didn't seem to notice the blood seeping through her short leather skirt. Star was fighting for her life and there was no room for anything else.

The dojo master would love her, I thought in awe. When Star fights, she's like the wind, totally empty. No past, no present, only now.

So I wasn't surprised when a sweating, bloodstained Star finally stood over her opponent, the point of her sword blade triumphantly grazing

Juno's throat.

'Kill, kill, kill!' chanted the crowd. Star had been fighting for them too. Now they wanted her to kill for them.

The gladiatrix stared calmly around the arena, as if she was genuinely considering the crowd's demands. Then she threw her sword down in the sand and raised a clenched fist. 'This is not Juno's day to die, citizens!' she cried in heavily accented Latin. 'She fought well. Spare her to fight another day!'

Reuben gave a gasp. I saw a bright drop of blood fall from Star's leather skirt into the sand; and another and another.

The gladiatrix swayed and clutched her side. She glanced down and looked astonished to see the spreading crimson stain. Without a sound, she crumpled to the ground, and lay totally still.

'NO!' I yelled.

I was on my feet before I'd thought. I was beside myself with distress. I'd just seen dozens of people senselessly murdered. But I didn't know them. I'd felt a connection with Star. She couldn't be *allowed* to die.

But someone was already vaulting over seats to get to her. It wasn't the lanista or a uniformed official. It was Orlando.

When I saw the look on his face, I felt myself falling through space. All these months I'd been waiting for this beautiful boy to realise I was his special someone. But he'd found her already and it wasn't me.

CHAPTER SEVEN

I hurled myself over the barrier and raced across the arena. I could feel grains of burning-hot sand stinging my bare legs as I ran. Down here, the smell of blood was suffocating.

Orlando was already kneeling beside Star. The lanista, Festus Brutus, limped hastily down from the stands to join Orlando. A doctor attached to the gladiator school hurried after him.

Star was trying to lift her head.

99

'Lie still!' Festus growled.

Orlando looked appalled to see me. 'Mel, what are you playing at? You're not supposed to be here.'

'Will Star be OK?' I asked in a small voice.

'Too early to say,' he said tersely. 'Now go and take care of Aurelia like you're supposed to.' A flicker of worry crossed his face. 'She's OK, isn't she?'

As OK as you can be when you've just watched thirty human beings slaughtered in public, I thought. But I just said huskily, 'She's fine.'

'Well, you shouldn't leave her too long.'

Star didn't look like a warrior queen lying there on the sand. She looked small and vulnerable. She's no taller than Aurelia, I thought.

But the gladiatrix was a warrior to the max. When the doctor ripped her blood-soaked skirt, Star didn't murmur, even though the leather was sticking to an open wound. The doctor began to probe the wound with metal instruments, trying to discover the extent of the damage. It must have been agony but she didn't flinch.

Up close I saw that Star's arms and legs were peppered with bruises and tiny healed scars. Through the slits of her mask, her closed eyelids were deathly pale.

'We should get her back to the barracks,' the doctor told Festus. 'She's lost a lot of blood.'

Orlando hovered anxiously. I wanted to believe his concern was strictly professional, but paranoid suspicions swarmed through my mind.

Had Orlando met Star on his previous trip and fallen head over heels-in-love with her? Did he organise his task force purely to save her from a bloody death in the arena? Was that why he couldn't tell us the purpose of the mission?

I stared down miserably at my rival. You were right, Melanie, I thought. Star's everything you'll never be. Sexy, fearless, mysterious . . .

Reuben came up behind me. 'You should come back,' he said. 'You can see Orlando's busy.'

'Give me a minute,' I pleaded.

Orlando and the lanista were helping the dazed gladiatrix to her feet, with some assistance from Juno. Between them they half-lifted, half-supported Star out of the arena. There were confused murmurings from the crowd.

I went back to my seat like a zombie.

'You missed my brother,' Aurelia said in a bright voice. 'He brought Titus Lucretius to meet me.'

'Didn't stay long, did they?' Reuben murmured in my ear. 'You'd almost think they'd been waiting to get her by herself.'

'So who was that beautiful boy you were talking to?' Aurelia asked me with that same fake brightness.

I could tell she totally wasn't thinking about what she was saying. She didn't know how I felt about Orlando. She couldn't know the last thing I needed right now was for him to have another female admirer.

Through my fog of misery I sensed that Aurelia's meeting with her future husband had distressed her. It was sweltering in the amphitheatre, but I saw her shiver. She drew her thin shawl more closely around her, and for the first time since I'd known her, she spoke like a haughty mistress addressing her slave. 'Find our bearers, Mella. I wish to leave. At once!'

*   *   *

That night I helped my mistress get ready for the banquet. I helped her put on her new silk stola. I arranged her hair and secured it with ornamental hairpins, making it look as if her complicated braids were studded with tiny pearls. She looked lovely when I'd finished, except for being so pale. She'd hardly said a word since we came back from the Games. I knew I should get her to open up and tell me what was wrong, but I was in a total daze. I was just going through the motions.

Being an angel isn't that different from being a gladiator, I thought bleakly. You might be bleeding inside, but you keep going. Your heart might be breaking, but you can't let it show.

Later, I ran about with the other house slaves, making our guests welcome. I brought warm scented water to wash the dust from their feet. I took ladies' shawls and gentlemen's cloaks. I plumped up the cushions on the couches, so our guests could recline like gods and goddesses, wearing their ceremonial crowns of leaves and flowers.

But none of it seemed real. Not like Orlando's face when he saw Star's blood soaking into the sand.

In the kitchen Reuben and two other slaves were helping with the preparations. Like all Roman kitchens, this one was a soot-encrusted hellhole. Can you believe Dorcas had to cook this entire banquet over a wood fire, with no windows for ventilation? Plus the dishes Quintus had selected for his guests were just *bizarre:* peacock eggs in pepper sauce, milk-fed snails sautéed with garlic, stuffed dormice. It was pretty obvious that Aurelia's brother hadn't designed his banquet to be enjoyed. He just wanted to impress his guests with how rich and important he was.

Reuben grabbed me as I tottered

past with a huge wine jug in each hand. 'OK, so Orlando has other things on his mind,' he said in a firm voice. 'And OK, so you're upset. But get over it. You're no good to Aurelia in this state and she's the one Orlando wants us to watch.'

'I can't help it, Reubs,' I wailed. 'It hurts so much.'

My angel buddy made me look at him. 'Maybe Mel Beeby can't get over it, but Helix can.'

Sometimes I think Reuben knows me better than anyone else in the universe. It's like he knew exactly the right thing to say. As he spoke my angel name out loud, my buddy's voice took on an amazingly powerful vibe. To my astonishment, I saw my name forming in the air in glowing letters, right there in that horrible kitchen. No one but Reubs and I saw, but I gasped. And guess what? I was over it! I snapped out of my self pity just like that. I wasn't Mel-with-a-broken-heart, I was an angel with a job to do. Reuben's right, I thought. I can do this. I'm going to do this.

I gave his hand a squeeze. It felt rough and calloused from his gardening, but still deeply comforting. 'Thanks, Sweetpea. I owe you.'

'I know,' Reuben agreed smugly. Without thinking he popped a nibble in his mouth and choked. 'What was that?'

'I hope it's not a stuffed dormouse!' I giggled.

I reached the dining room to hear a slave announcing solemnly, 'Quintus Flavius and Titus Lucretius!'

I'd had my suspicions about Quintus as you know, and the minute he walked into the room, I knew I'd been right. Quintus was handsome, even charming, but you could see an unmistakable glint of cruelty in his eyes.

Aurelia's future husband followed him in. He was short and squat and his lips looked unpleasantly red through his beard. He handed me his cloak. 'Well, well. It's the little slave girl,' he said in a high thin voice.

I almost fainted with terror. I knew this guy. I'd breathed his icky alcohol fumes. I'd felt his pervy vibes touch my angelic energy field. Omigosh! I thought. Titus Lucretius was our intruder!!

I wanted to grab Aurelia and run right out of that creepy house and keep running until we ended up somewhere nice and normal.

I was scared and disgusted, but I was angry too. Titus could have arranged to meet my mistress, if that's all he'd wanted. But he didn't want to get to know Aurelia as a person, did he? He wanted to creep up on her in the dark like she was his helpless prey. He wanted power over her.

Aurelia's brother must have been in on it, I thought in horror. That's how Titus got past the watchman. Ugh, this era is SO sick!

I was so upset I had to rush off to update Reuben.

Dorcas was standing over the hearth, simmering what looked like little grey bird-tongues in some kind of strange spicy sauce. The slave woman turned in surprise as I burst in, and saw my stricken expression. 'You've seen The

Knife then,' she said grimly.

It turned out that Dorcas knew exactly what was going on, and it sickened her to the core. 'Titus Lucretius is the head of Nero's secret police,' she told us in a low voice. 'We call him The Knife because he's had so many people murdered.'

'Aurelia can't possibly marry him,' I gasped. 'Someone's got to stop it.'

Dorcas shook her head. 'Everyone's too scared of him. I just thank the gods my mistress never saw this day. She loved that poor girl like her own.' She wiped her eyes on her apron. 'You two genuinely care about her, don't you?' she said in a puzzled voice.

I nodded. 'Yes, we do.'

'You'd better go back before anyone gets suspicious. Here, take this to Titus Lucretius.' The slave woman ladled out more mulled wine. Then she pursed her lips and spat deliberately into the jug. 'A little present from the people,' she whispered.

Quintus and his guests were tucking into their peacocks' eggs. The guests had brought their personal slaves to wait on them. If they didn't like something they simply threw it on the floor and the slaves obediently swooped and picked it up.

Once I looked up to see Aurelia's father in the doorway in his freshly-ironed toga, looking dazed. But when he saw his adopted daughter reclining on a couch next to the chief of Rome's secret police, he went away.

I'd have been ashamed too, if I was him. Aurelia's dad was the one person who could have put a stop to this, but he'd given away his authority to his son, and everyone knew it.

My mistress had left her huge egg untouched on her plate. She didn't eat any of the next course either. She looked dangerously close to tears. This feast was meant to be an opportunity for her and Titus to get to know each other, but both he and Quintus were treating her as if she didn't exist. They just giggled together at private jokes, like cruel little schoolboys. It's like they were deliberately trying to humiliate her.

I went to take Aurelia's plate,

thinking I could whisper something comforting in her ear. Suddenly Titus caught my wrist in his clammy grip. I noticed guests watching us with unpleasant expressions. For a moment, their faces seemed to distort in the lamplight, as if they might be going to morph at any moment into something totally evil.

I went utterly cold. Brice had been telling the truth. Some of these Romans weren't actually human.

'Your mistress doesn't seem to be enjoying her flamingo tongues,' Titus was saying in his high voice. 'Perhaps she's grown too used to barbarian cuisine. Has Aurelia Flavia turned into a barbarian? What's your opinion, girl?'

The PODS guests waited with interest to hear what I'd say. They knew who I was and I knew who they were. But they couldn't exactly blow their cover, and I certainly couldn't blow mine, so we all kept up the pretence that everyone here was human.

'My mistress is not hungry,' I told him defiantly.

Titus and Quintus looked at each other. 'Then maybe your mistress is thirsty!' Giggling like a spiteful little kid, Titus lifted his goblet and threw its contents all over her, absolutely soaking her dress.

For a moment Aurelia just stared blankly at the spreading crimson stain, and I knew she was remembering Star, bleeding from her wounds in the arena. Then with great dignity, she drew her silk shawl around her. 'And you want me to marry this man?' she said to her brother in a trembling voice. She rose from her couch and left the room. As I rushed after her, shouts of laughter followed us.

Now I knew why Orlando had planted me in this house. The PODS wanted to destroy Aurelia. They didn't just want to harm her physically. They wanted to kill her spirit.

But why on earth would they bother, unless she threatened their own malevolent plans in some way? And that was just ridiculous. Aurelia wasn't a threat to anybody. She's just a sweet girl, I thought. A sweet, harmless little rich girl.

*   *   *

I shot out of an uneasy doze to hear my mistress moving around in the dark. I opened my eyes as she crept softly out of the room. Probably just going to the latrine, I thought drowsily.

Erm, so why is she wearing her cloak, Melanie? I asked myself.

I was off my couch in a flash. I was Helix, an angelic trouble-shooter on a mission that was just about to go seriously pearshaped.

You should have seen this coming, babe, I scolded myself. That banquet gave Aurelia a nightmare preview of her future. Now she's rushing off to the arms of her secret love.

I beamed urgent signals to Reuben as I threw on my clothes.

Meet me under the quince tree, Sweetpea. NOW.

Outside, the warm night air smelled of roses. A perfect full moon sailed

112

over the quince tree. Reuben came hopping out of the slave quarters, still trying to buckle his sandals. 'I'd have been here quicker but I had to shut Minerva in her kennel,' he whispered. 'What's up?'

'Aurelia's running away. I think she's going to this guy. We've got to follow her.'

We slipped out of the slaves' entrance and raced along the dark street. 'This is terrible, Reubs!' I panted out. 'You heard what Dorcas said. Anyone who gets in Titus's way ends up seriously dead. If he finds out about her boyfriend, Aurelia could be next.'

'We don't even know she's got a boyfriend,' Reuben objected breathlessly. 'This might not be what you think.'

'Why else would a nice Roman girl be out in the streets at night? She's not likely to be going clubbing!'

'There she is!' said Reuben suddenly.

Aurelia had stopped to peer at a piece of papyrus in the moonlight. We silently caught her up.

'Right at the crossroads,' she murmured. 'Take the third on the right by the olive mill. Go to the old aqueduct and wait.'

And she was off again.

When we reached the aqueduct, someone stepped out of the shadows. With a flicker of alarm, I saw other figures moving behind him. I heard someone whisper, 'Bless you little sister,' then they all set off together down the street.

Hello, I thought. 'This isn't about some boyfriend is it?' I whispered to Reubs.

'Doesn't look like it,' he agreed.

Other anonymous humans joined them as they hurried along. It went on like this, a growing crowd of silent men and women, all heading for the same unknown destination. Now and then one would stop and listen intently, to see if they were being followed, then they'd hurry on.

Finally we reached open ground. There had been houses here once, but they had crumbled into rubble years ago. We trailed Aurelia and her companions through the moonlit ruins until we came to an overgrown fig tree. The gnarled branches partly concealed a low archway, which had once been part of a temple. Everyone silently filed inside. When we were quite sure the coast was clear, we followed.

On the other side of the arch, a flight of steep stone steps disappeared down into the dark. On every sixth or seventh step, someone had placed a lighted clay lamp.

Helix might be up for it, but Mel Beeby wasn't too keen to go exploring some crumbly old crypt in the dark, so I quickly helped myself to a lamp.

It's lucky I did. At the bottom we found ourselves in a low stone tunnel with dozens of other tunnels going off. It was a total labyrinth.

'Now what do we do?' My voice echoed spookily around the tunnel.

Reuben pointed at the wall. 'We could always follow the fish.'

By the flickery flame of my lamp, I saw a crudely painted fish daubed on the tunnel wall. 'That's like the one I saw on Aurelia's letter,' I said in amazement. Reuben had been right, as we crept along the tunnel the fish symbol reappeared at intervals, wherever the tunnel branched off.

'What's that sound!' my buddy asked.

I strained my ears. It sounded like the blurry murmuring of bees. What IS going on down here, I wondered nervously?

The tunnel went on and on. Sometimes the murmuring seemed quite close, then it would fade again. Each time it grew louder, the back of my neck went strangely tingly.

All at once I smelled incense. Not the stuff Romans used in temples. This was musky and sweet like burning pine cones. The bee-sound was getting really powerful now. In fact it was giving me goosebumps. For the first time I realised the murmuring had words. It wasn't Latin. It was unlike any language I'd ever heard.

Next minute the tunnel opened out into an underground chamber. I glimpsed more wall paintings, strange and richly coloured. Then I saw the rapt lamplit faces of hundreds of humans.

My heart practically jumped into my mouth. I'd seen people in this state on TV: eyes closed, hands raised, chanting, swaying. And if it wasn't drugs, a fake guru was always involved. I scanned the ecstatic faces, anxiously, until I found Aurelia. Don't let this be happening, I prayed. Then I saw her, swaying and chanting along with everyone else.

'This is SO much worse than I thought!' I gasped.

I grabbed Reuben's hand and dragged him out.

'What are you so upset about?' he asked in a grumpy voice. 'The chanting was cool. The total opposite of that arena.'

'Sweetpea, I'm not being horrible, but you haven't been to Earth that often, so you've probably never heard of religious cults. Well what we just saw, that's a cult. I don't know how Aurelia got sucked into it. Maybe they had a secret chapter in Ancient Britain or something. But she's in real danger. We're in way over our heads, Reubs. We've got to tell Orlando.'

'You're the expert,' he sighed.

'This incense is making my nose run,' I said. 'Let's wait outside.'

*   *   *

Next day, using the excuse of taking Aurelia's wine-stained stola to the fullers, (a kind of Roman dry cleaners) Reuben and I hired a litter to take us to the ludus.

The gladiator school was basically a kind of Roman boot camp, with high walls set with metal spikes and broken pottery, and prowling heavies everywhere. Few people actually wanted to be gladiators, so to stop his protégées escaping, Festus Brutus had them watched twenty-four seven.

We found Orlando and the lanista behind the barracks, drilling a sullen group of human recruits in a make-shift arena.

Everyone but Orlando and Festus had thick protective padding tied around their arms and legs. The recruits were supposed to charge at straw men, with wooden swords, and pretend to disembowel them. Under Festus's scowling gaze, Orlando made them charge again and again, until he was satisfied with their technique.

'Orlando is something else,' grinned Reuben. 'He's been here two weeks, max, and he's already like Festus Brutus's right-hand man.'

'I don't know how he does it,' I agreed.

Reuben and I rushed up to Orlando at the end of the session.

'I don't believe you two,' he sighed. 'You'd better have a really good reason for coming here. It's taken days to get Festus Brutus to trust me. If he sees you guys, he'll go up the wall.'

'We have got a good reason,' I babbled urgently. 'Aurelia's joined a dangerous cult.'

Orlando didn't react at all how I'd expected. In fact he laughed with pure relief. 'You followed her to the catacombs, right?'

I stared at him in consternation.

'You know about that place?'

'Of course!' he said. 'It's the only place Christians can meet in safety. Practising the Christian faith is illegal in Nero's time.'

My mouth dropped open. 'Those people were Christians?'

'They can only meet in secret. That's why they use symbols, like the fish, so only insiders understand what's being passed on.'

My cheeks burned with embarrassment. *You are SO ignorant, Melanie!* I scolded myself. *Kindergarten angels know more than you.*

Reuben looked worried. 'What would happen if they were found out?'

Orlando glanced away. 'They'd be put to death.'

'Are you serious?' I gasped. 'That girl is in enough trouble as it is! We just found out her brother is marrying her off to this evil secret police chief.'

Orlando nodded. 'The Knife.'

'Omigosh, you knew!' *Of course he did, you birdbrain, that's why he asked you to take care of her, Melanie, I* reminded myself.

I suddenly remembered something. 'Erm, how's Star?'

Orlando's eyes softened. 'She's making a good recovery. Festus Brutus took her into his own home, so she can be cared for properly.'

Well, he wouldn't want to lose his investment, I thought darkly.

*   *   *

All the way home, I thought about how I'd underestimated Aurelia. 'A sweet harmless rich girl', I'd called her. My prejudice had blinded me to all kinds of obvious clues. Her hatred of all forms of cruelty. Her kindness to people worse off than herself. Her talk of souls.

I waited until bedtime, when Aurelia and I were alone together in her room, and then I told her that Reubs and me knew her secret and would do everything in our power to protect her.

My mistress jumped up in terror, knocking over the jar of almond oil, and spilling the sweet-scented oil

121

everywhere. 'You've been spying on me, Mella! I trusted you and you betrayed me.'

'You still can trust me, I swear!' I told her. 'Reuben and I only followed you because we were so worried about you.' And I explained how we'd decided she had a secret sweetheart.

Aurelia must have sensed that my words came straight from the heart, because she looked deep into my eyes and it was a total replay of our first meeting at the slave market. It was like she *knew*. But at the same time she didn't. My mistress sat down again without a word, and I continued brushing her hair.

'Your mum was a Christian too, wasn't she?' I said.

'She gave me this.' Aurelia took off her bulla. 'Look at the back.'

On the reverse of her charm was a tiny mother of pearl cross.

My eyes filled with tears. Aurelia had picked a really lonely way to be true to herself. Then I thought, but she's not alone any more.

I caught Aurelia watching me in the

polished bronze mirror. 'I never knew there were friends like you,' she said softly. 'One day I'll give you your freedom.'

My freedom wasn't in her hands, but Aurelia wasn't to know that.

We talked into the night, and as I blew out the lamp, we agreed that we were both happier than we'd been for days.

We weren't to know that every word of our conversation had been overheard by Aurelia's brother, adviser to the Emperor Nero and faithful servant to the Powers of Darkness.

CHAPTER EIGHT

I woke to find lamplight flickering confusingly in my eyes.

Dorcas was shaking me. 'Get dressed!' she said in a fierce whisper. 'Leave this house and take Aurelia Flavia with you.'

Aurelia rubbed her eyes drowsily. 'Is there a fire?'

'You've been betrayed, little mistress,' Dorcas told her. 'Your brother has found out you follow the teacher from Nazareth.'

We jumped up and began to fling on our clothes.

'Why are you helping me, Dorcas?' Aurelia said from inside her tunic. 'You still follow the old gods.'

'I follow my heart,' said Dorcas in a low voice. 'They say a teacher who says such things must be insane. But I say his is a better madness than Nero's.'

We were still dressing frantically, when we heard the sound of tramping feet outside. The Praetorian Guard, Nero's police, had come to arrest us.

Reuben came running as soon as he heard the commotion, so they arrested him too.

Aurelia's father watched it all from the door of his study. 'I showed her nothing but kindness and she betrayed me,' he said in disgust.

'I love you, Pater,' Aurelia called desperately. 'I always loved you!'

I heard desolate howls from Minerva's kennel as we were led away.

The guards marched us through the early morning streets, I could see Aurelia was in a state of shock. She kept looking around, wide-eyed, as if she totally hadn't realised how beautiful the world was until this moment. The sun was rising and birds sang joyfully from hidden gardens. The air was full of scents, roses from the flower market, eye-watering fumes from the street of the leather workers, burning incense from a shrine. I was trying hard not to think about what would happen when we stopped marching and reached our destination. I just put one foot in front of the other; left right, left right.

People called out to know why we'd been arrested. 'We bagged a few more Christians!' a guard shouted back cheerfully. The mood immediately darkened. 'Filthy vermin,' a woman screamed. One man spat in our faces. 'You're going to die today, Christian scum!'

Outside one semi-derelict apartment block, people pelted us with rotting fruit, and someone started throwing stones. Everyone loathed and despised us, the guards included.

'I don't understand people like you,' a guard said contemptuously to Aurelia. 'We've got perfectly good Roman gods and goddesses. But you have to have your own special god, it makes me sick.'

'Why do you care which god she worships, man?' Reuben asked. 'She's not dissing yours, is she?'

'Reuben!' I hissed. 'You're not meant to hold philosophical discussions with the guards.'

'All Christians are in league with the barbarian hordes,' the guard ranted on. 'You want to burn Rome down around our ears.'

When we reached the amphitheatre, crowds of Romans were already queuing to go in. We were taken to a row of cells and a guard booted us in through a door. I just had time to see the gruesome straw on the floor, then the door slammed behind us and we were plunged into total darkness.

We're going to be fine, I told myself bravely. Any minute now that door will open and Orlando will walk in.

But when we finally heard the bolts being dragged back, some hours later, a security guy stood in the doorway, grinning unpleasantly. 'Let's be having you!' he said. 'Mustn't keep those hungry pussy cats waiting.'

'No,' leered his mate, 'we've been starving them specially.'

Other Christians were being dragged from neighbouring cells. We were chained together like dangerous criminals and kicked and prodded along a low gloomy tunnel. We stumbled along, our eyes fixed on the white blaze of sunlight at the far end. Fifty-thousand brutal voices surged to meet us. They were all chanting the same word over and over. 'Kill! Kill! Kill!'

Aurelia stumbled and Reuben and I quickly steadied her. 'I know it doesn't seem like it, but we're going to be OK,' I told her.

My mistress's voice trembled, but her face was totally calm. 'Other martyrs have died for their faith,' she said bravely. 'And I know I will soon be reunited with my mother in Heaven.'

When the crowd saw us emerge, blinking and confused in the pitiless midday sun, they howled with excitement.

I'd been clinging to the hope that Orlando would stage some fabulous last-minute rescue. If so, he was leaving it desperately late.

I stared wildly around the amphitheatre. Where were all the angels? I wondered.

Two gates flew open and thirty or more lions exploded into the arena. I assumed they were lions. I just heard furious roars and saw a mad blur of gold. Then my world went into slow-mo, and suddenly everything was in nightmare close-up; wild yellow eyes with tawny flecks, fleshy crimson tongues. Bared fangs drooling saliva.

When I smelled their hot breath on my face, I squeezed my eyes shut and flung my arms around Aurelia. It was the only way I could think of to protect her; some crazy idea that I could at least slow the ravenous beasts down. In that moment I relived every piece of wildlife film footage featuring lions and helpless baby animals I'd ever seen on TV. I didn't just see it. I was getting Dolby surround sound. The juicy ripping of muscle. The splintering of bone . . .

But the seconds ticked by and there was no ripping or splintering.

The crowd had gone oddly silent. Even the lions had gone quiet. Their roaring had been replaced by a bizarre rumbling, like the throbbing engines of a very old bus. Amazed laughter rippled round the amphitheatre.

I opened my eyes. It was like a scene from a particularly magical dream. My angel buddy was standing in the centre of a circle of lions, completely unharmed. The beasts gazed back at him with adoring expressions. The rumbling was the purring of thirty blissed-out lions.

Aurelia was trembling with awe. 'It's a miracle!' she breathed.

When will you ever learn, Mel Beeby? I asked myself. We ARE the angels. We didn't need any help.

And at that moment the audience

129

went wild. All around the amphitheatre, Romans jumped to their feet: slaves, citizens, senators, men, women and children. And all because of a honey-coloured angel-boy with dreads. Omigosh, they love him, I thought tearfully. They love him even though they think he's a Christian!

Hang on? A worrying thought occurred to me. Shouldn't all these people have their thumbs UP?

But no matter where I looked, people were jabbing their thumbs in a sharp and quite unmistakable downward direction.

They still want us to die! I thought in despair. Then my heart gave a leap as I heard everyone yelling. 'FREE THEM! FREE THEM!!'

That's when I found out the Hollywood movies got it wrong. In Roman times, the thumbs-up gesture actually meant, 'Stab him in the jugular!'.

An official in a toga approached the barrier, keeping as far away as possible from the lions. 'Hey, you kids! Get over here,' he called. 'His Imperial Majesty wants to meet you.'

'Omigosh, Nero's here at the Games!' I squeaked.

Normally I'd have panicked at the prospect of meeting a real live emperor, particularly an emperor as cruel and decadent as Nero, but we'd just survived wild lions, as you know, so we were up for anything.

We were marched into the Emperor's presence between hefty Praetorian guards.

Considering he was the head of the biggest empire the ancient world had ever known, Nero wasn't actually that impressive. He had practically no chin to speak of and his eyes were such a pale blue, that you could hardly detect the colour. He was wearing what appeared to be an old dressing-gown spattered with stains and crusty splodges of food.

He might not have the looks or the gorgeous robes, but Nero had the imperial attitude all right. His gaze flickered over me and Aurelia, as if we were little dung beetles, unworthy of his attention. Then he saw Reuben, and a greedy glitter lit up his eyes. 'We live in strange times,' he said. 'So strange that the mighty Nero is willing to make a bargain with a Christian slave boy. Teach me how to make lions love me, and I'll let you and your little girlfriends go free.'

I understood where Nero was coming from. He'd just witnessed a despised slave perform a feat that no ordinary human could possibly have done, not even an all-powerful emperor. Now he wanted this magical gift for himself. If Nero could get wild lions to worship him, his people would think he was some kind of god!

Of course, that was never going to happen. Reuben was firm in the way only a pure angel can be. 'Sorry, that won't be possible,' he said politely.

I'd have said the Emperor was borderline normal up till this point. But the instant Reubs turned him down, I felt him switch.

Nero didn't froth at the mouth, or rant, he just went very very still. But you could feel this terrible darkness seething inside him.

'Take them out of my sight!' he commanded the guards. 'They bore me.'

Aurelia gasped. 'But what will happen to us?'

'I haven't decided,' said the Emperor in an irritated voice. 'But throwing you to wild animals is obviously out. What do you think, my friends?' he called over his shoulder.

My heart sank as Titus and Quintus hurried forward. Nero drew them into a huddle. 'How shall I kill the Christian children?' he asked petulantly.

'Easy!' said Titus in his high voice. 'Put them in the ring with trained gladiators!'

The Emperor let out a mad titter of laughter. 'Excellent! Take them to the dungeons. Tomorrow the gods can decide their fate.'

CHAPTER NINE

The sun was setting as the guards marched us through the city. In households all over Rome, people were cooking their suppers. The air was hazy with wood-smoke and I kept catching savoury whiffs of frying fish and onions. Once I saw a woman on a balcony, hushing her new baby to sleep.

As we tramped through twilit streets, the Christians sang to keep up their spirits. Early Christian hymns were v. uplifting, nothing like the dirges we sang at my comprehensive. Reuben and I totally couldn't help joining in. Then we taught them Reuben's song, *We're not alone.* The Christians soon picked it up and put a cool little Roman spin on it. But we were starting to attract attention and the guards got nervous and told us to shut up.

As we were passing the Temple of Vesta, I felt an unmistakable mystical tingle. A door stood open between two lofty stone pillars. I caught a glimpse of

134

a rich velvety darkness inside, and the golden flicker of the sacred flame. The sweet smell of incense wafted towards me.

Suddenly, I had to pinch myself. Coming down the steps towards me in the tunic and veil of a Vestal virgin, was ANOTHER Aurelia!

For an instant everything seemed to shimmer: the girl in her gauzy white veil, the beautiful temple, the violet sky with its pinpricks of stars—then Aurelia's double vanished into the crowd like a dream.

Typical Melanie, I had to blurt out what I'd seen. 'Omigosh, Aurelia! I've just seen your absolute spitting image!!'

'No talking!' barked one of the guards.

Aurelia looked bewildered. 'You saw someone who looks like me?' she whispered.

'She's so like you it's spooky,' I whispered back. 'And she's a Vestal virgin, just like you once wanted to be. Isn't that amazing?'

She stared at me wide-eyed.

'That must be why you always felt something was missing,' I told her excitedly. 'Perhaps you really are a twin!'

Aurelia's eyes brimmed with tears. 'Perhaps,' she said softly. 'But even if you're right, I'm not going to live long enough to meet her.'

'No, it's all going to work out, I swear!' I promised. 'I can feel it, Aurelia! It's like, there's this beautiful mosaic forming and we're all a part of it, but we're too close to see the pattern.'

I really meant it. I could feel all the gorgeous multicoloured pieces coming together around us. Of course, I had no idea how complex this particular mosaic would turn out to be . . .

*   *   *

That night Orlando sprang us from the dungeons. I have NO idea how he got hold of those Praetorian guard uniforms but my angelic colleagues made brilliantly convincing guardsmen.

No one even challenged us! The real

guards were totally convinced that their dungeons were impregnable, so they were just chilling out in the guard-room, drinking wine and playing backgammon. We basically sneaked out right under their noses!

The Christians naturally assumed that Orlando and his team belonged to the early Christian underground. They thanked him and quickly melted away into the night.

'We'd better lie low,' I told Orlando. 'By tomorrow every Praetorian guard in this city will be looking for us, not to mention Nero's secret police.'

'We're taking you back to the ludus with us,' said Orlando. 'We've got a wagon waiting a couple of streets away.'

'But the minute Festus Brutus sees us, he'll turn us over to the authorities,' I objected.

'You're wrong,' said Orlando. 'It was Festus who lent us the wagon. He might seem rough and ready, but his heart is in the right place.'

Aurelia was chatting to some of our rescuers, so I took the opportunity to tell Orlando about my amazing discovery. 'I saw this girl on the way here,' I said eagerly. 'She's a Vestal virgin at the temple and I'm not exaggerating, she could be Aurelia's identical twin!!'

My voice faded as I saw Orlando's expression. He knew, I thought. Orlando had known Aurelia had a twin all along.

*   *   *

The lanista lived in a comfortable apartment behind the training school. A slave showed us into a brightly-painted room where Festus Brutus was doing Roman-style calculations at his desk. A grizzled old dog lay at his feet, looking as bad-tempered and battle-scarred as the lanista himself.

'Just a minute,' Festus barked as we came in. 'These taxes will be the death of me.'

We waited while he finished scribbling numerals on a wax tablet with a sharp metal stylus. I looked around with cautious interest. There was a couch heaped with leopard and zebra skins, probably booty from various games. All around the walls, an artist had painted scenes of gory gladiatorial combat. Alongside the usual offerings in the household shrine, was a simple wooden sword. I knew from Reuben that this was a 'rudis'. A lanista would give this symbolic sword to a gladiator on the day he finally bought his freedom.

You're such a ditz, Mel, I told myself. Festus Brutus wasn't wounded on the battlefield at all. He got those injuries in the arena. Festus had been a gladiator too!

He looked up at last, rubbing bloodshot eyes. 'Well, well, if it isn't the lion children!' he growled. 'The city is buzzing like a beehive with news of your—' He broke off abruptly. He was staring at Aurelia with a stunned expression. 'But she's exactly like—'

Orlando quickly shook his head and Festus checked himself.

'My friends would like to see Star,' said Orlando. 'If it isn't too late.'

The old gladiator gave an amazed

laugh. 'I'm getting senile,' he muttered. 'Aiding and abetting religious dissidents. Giving new cadets the run of my ludus. Next thing I'll be turning Christian.'

You couldn't blame him for being confused. He had no idea why he'd allowed this barbarian slave to wander freely around Rome, instead of keeping him chained in his barracks like a dog. But we did.

Festus, like Aurelia, was deeply susceptible to angelic vibes. Plus, I have to say, Orlando is excellent at his job!

We followed Festus Brutus across a moonlit courtyard to the small apartment where the gladiatrix was convalescing.

'Is Star any better?' I asked.

'For someone who almost bled to death, she's alarmingly well,' he said in a grumbling voice. 'That girl has unnatural powers of recovery.'

Beside the open door was a peach tree so weighed down with fruit, that its branches almost touched the ground. Soft voices floated out of the house into the evening air. Star sat with her back to us in a flood of lamplight. Juno stood behind her, plaiting Star's hair.

It's never one thing that makes you recognise a person. It's more like lots of small things. A tone of voice. A gesture. The texture of someone's hair.

Festus gave a last baffled glance at Aurelia. 'Strange times indeed,' he murmured. He picked up a fallen peach, dusted it off on his tunic, and took a bite. 'You have a visitor!' he called to Star.

'I am not interested in visitors,' the gladiatrix called back in her foreign-sounding Latin.

'You'll be interested in this one,' said Festus.

There was a strange excitement in his voice.

But by this time I knew. I hadn't been looking for similarities before. I'd been confused by Star's mask and her sexy fighting costume, not to mention my own mixed-up emotions. But now I knew with absolute certainty what I'd see when Star turned to face us; a girl with grey eyes, flyaway brown hair, and a dimple in her cheek.

My mistress wasn't separated from one sister at birth, but two. The Christian girl, the Vestal virgin and the feisty gladiatrix were identical triplets!

I'll probably never see two humans more astonished than Aurelia and Star when they finally set eyes on each other.

First they were stunned, then disbelieving, then shocked. Then they flew to each other, squealing like little kids on Christmas morning. They hugged and cried all over each other, kissing each other's hands and cheeks.

'I used to see you in my dreams,' Aurelia wept.

Tears streamed down Star's face. 'I saw you too!' she sobbed. 'I knew you were real. But they beat me and told me it wasn't true!'

'Omigosh,' I whispered to Orlando. 'They've been communicating telepathically all these years!!'

'Let's leave them,' he whispered to me and Reubs. 'They've got some serious catching up to do.'

Festus Brutus had vanished tactfully

into his house, loudly blowing his nose.

The three of us went to sit under an olive tree in a white pool of moonlight. At first we were all too moved to talk. It felt a bit weird sitting so close to Orlando in the dark, but I just looked up at the night sky and listened to the cicadas singing somewhere in the bushes. I sensed that Orlando had something on his mind. Eventually he cleared his throat. 'I think it's time I told you about the curse.'

My mouth fell open. 'No way! There's a curse? As well as triplets!'

I think I already mentioned the Roman tendency to curse everyone and everything that annoyed them. But the curse Orlando was talking about was in a totally different league.

'Ancient Romans see signs and portents in everything, as you know,' he told us. 'If you spill wine at a banquet, you'll have bad luck in business. If your child is born with a harelip, it's because you're being punished by the gods. In such a superstitious climate, even the birth of twin babies is seen as alarming.

Surviving triplets are so unique that their very existence seems unnatural.'

I could tell we were going to be here quite a while, so I made myself comfortable against the nubbly trunk of the olive tree and listened to Orlando's story.

'Fifteen years ago, in the poorest part of Rome, a woman gave birth to three identical baby girls. After a long, difficult labour she was too weak to hold her baby daughters in her arms. She died only hours after giving birth. These children weren't just linked by the circumstances of their birth,' Orlando explained. 'Their souls were connected too.'

'Omigosh, they were spiritual triplets!' I gasped. 'That is SO special!'

Orlando nodded. 'Our Agency had been expecting three very special children to show up during this era. They just didn't know exactly where or when. Unfortunately the local Opposition agent was quicker off the mark, and he grabbed the opportunity to do major cosmic damage.'

A passing moth brushed against my

bare arm, making me shiver. 'Go on,' I whispered.

'OK, now you guys know from Dark Studies that a curse is basically a negative thought, delivered with intense force?'

Reuben and I nodded nervously.

'But if enough humans feed it with the energy of belief, a curse can become a kind of black hole, sucking in more and more negativity, until eventually it takes on a demonic life of its own.'

Reuben swallowed. 'That sounds dark.'

'It gets darker, believe me,' said Orlando. 'Like most uneducated Romans, the triplets' grandmother was terrified of what she couldn't understand. She had been jealous of her daughter-in-law, and was furious that her son expected her to feed and care for these three freakish infants. This made her a perfect target for the Opposition.'

'Oh-oh,' I said.

'This jealous old woman was convinced that the triplets' mother must have offended the gods, and she made up her mind to free herself and her son from this bad luck. She bought a live chicken and took it to the shrine of a particularly unsavoury underworld god. A Dark agent, posing as a priest, accepted her offering. She started to weep and wring her hands, so he made her tell him what was wrong, and after he'd heard her story, this fake priest told her that he knew a way to divert the bad luck from her son's house.'

'Don't tell me—with a curse,' said Reuben.

'Yes, with a curse. Since the old woman was illiterate, he promised to help her word the curse to make it binding.'

Orlando described how the fake priest scratched the words on a special curse tablet made of lead, and watched with a strange eagerness as the triplets' grandmother placed it in the bloodstained shrine.

'What did the curse say?' I whispered.

'That the unnatural babies must be taken from the house and abandoned in three different areas of the city, where they would be exposed to the elements and left to die. If the old woman did everything exactly as she was told, she and her son would prosper in all their dealings. But if the girls were ever *reunited,* not only would this good fortune end, Rome itself would fall.

'While her son was sleeping, the grandmother took the new-born girls out of the house under cover of darkness and abandoned them in different areas of the city, as she'd been instructed. By this time, the local light agents had got their act together. With a little celestial help, two of the triplets quickly found new families. But despite our agents' best efforts, the third—Star—was left crying in an alleyway for three days before any human noticed.'

Reuben was horrified. 'It's a wonder she survived.'

'You'd be surprised. New-born humans are surprisingly tough,' said Orlando.

Orlando described how Star was

eventually rescued—if you can call it that—by the owner of a sleazy public house called *The Pomegranate*. But when she was three years old, this charming guy sold her on to a slave dealer. After that, Star basically spent her childhood running away from abusive owners, and being recaptured.

It's not surprising that she grew into a little female hooligan, who hit first and asked questions afterwards. Yet like her sisters, she had a strong spiritual side. She had vivid dreams and saw strange visions. But Star learned it was unwise to talk about these things. She decided it was better to be laughed at for being a feisty tomboy, than stoned as a witch. When she was ten years old, she stowed away on a ship bound for Carthage, to seek her fortune.

I shivered when Orlando told us this. How weird is that? It's like when I made up my fictional life-story for Aurelia, I had somehow tapped into Star's real life-story.

Star did find her fortune; kind of. Soon after she arrived, a sharp-eyed local lanista noticed a wild-haired ragamuffin defending herself in the street from some older boys. He was impressed by her spirit and thought it would be amusing to train her for the arena.

Reuben looked disgusted. 'He wanted to put a ten-year-old girl in the arena? That is SO sick.'

Orlando shook his head. 'Star doesn't see it that way. She says it was the first time anyone ever believed in her. Festus Brutus saw her fight a few weeks ago and decided to buy her for his ludus. To begin with he was just exploiting her like everyone else, but now I think he genuinely wants to help Star to buy her freedom.'

'Who gave her that name?' I asked curiously.

'Star was called dozens of different names while she was growing up, but none of them were her own. So when she needed a stage name, she decided to call herself Star, her private name for herself when she was a small slave girl,' Orlando explained.

I felt my eyes prickle with tears. I

couldn't imagine how that unloved child had survived such a harsh life.

'What about the other sister? The temple girl?' asked Reuben.

Orlando smiled, 'Lucilla is something else. Her foster parents never told her of the circumstances of her birth, yet she always knew that she had an unusual destiny. From the age of three or four, she'd plead with her parents to take her to the Temple of Vesta. If they refused, Lucilla ran off there by herself, taking offerings of flowers and cakes. She told her parents she felt peaceful there. No-one was surprised when the temple authorities sought her out to train her as a Vestal virgin.'

'So now all three sisters are in Rome,' Reuben remarked. 'Star returned from Carthage or wherever. Aurelia just got back from Britain, and Lucilla was here all along.'

'Lucilla will be so amazed when she finds out she's got two long lost sisters,' I said excitedly.

Reuben frowned. 'But won't it be dangerous to bring them together?'

'Omigosh, the curse!' I gasped. 'I forgot about that.'

Orlando shook his head. 'The three sisters are supposed to be reunited. That's been our objective all along.'

'Orlando, that is SO cool!' I was practically hugging myself.

Orlando had the funny look he gets when I've missed the point. 'This isn't some family reunion, Mel,' he said in a patient voice. 'Or the Agency would never have backed our mission.'

'No, of course not,' I said hastily.

'It's an event of major cosmic significance,' he explained. 'Individually, all the girls have wonderful qualities, yet until now they've been incomplete. But once they are reunited, their inner light will become so powerful, that it will shine down the centuries.' Orlando fixed me with his most intense expression. 'These girls will transform history, Mel.'

Reuben looked nervous. 'Do the PODS know about this?'

'Why do you think they tried to keep them apart?' said Orlando softly.

I felt a sudden pang of worry. 'We should go to the temple,' I told him. 'We should go and find Lucilla now!'

*   *   *

The Powers of Darkness had other ideas. On the way to the Temple of Vesta we ran into every Roman obstacle imaginable: builders' wagons blocking the street, floods from burst water pipes. We even got stopped by two night watchmen with leather buckets, wanting to know if anyone had reported a fire. But finally we were racing up the long flight of temple steps, taking them two and three at a time.

When we reached the top, a shiver went through me as if someone was walking on my grave. The door to the temple stood wide open. We rushed inside, but Lucilla and the other Vestals were nowhere to be seen. The shrine to the goddess was in darkness, its sacred flame totally snuffed out.

CHAPTER TEN

Vesta's lamp lay smashed into pieces at the far end of the temple. It was obvious it had been hurled there by a supernatural force.

Reuben silently collected the glimmering gold fragments and returned them to the altar. It was a sweet Reuben-type gesture, as if he was apologising personally to the goddess.

Without her sacred flame burning on the altar, Vesta's temple felt like a lifeless shell. Orlando gazed around him in despair. 'It's over,' he said in a dull voice.

'It isn't over,' Reuben comforted him. 'It's just a—a bad setback.'

'It's a disaster,' said Orlando huskily. 'The Dark forces got Lucilla and it's all my fault.'

'We'll find her,' I said, with more confidence than I felt.

Reuben shook his head. 'We can't leave the temple like this. Every evil entity in Ancient Rome will think they've got squatter's rights.'

But Orlando was on his way out of the door. 'Sorry, I've got to go,' he said miserably. 'I've got to figure out what to do next.' He hurried off into the night.

Until this moment, I'd put Orlando on a pedestal. Now for the first time I saw how vulnerable he was.

'It's no wonder Orlando's stressing out,' I said miserably. 'This mission is too much responsibility for one trainee.'

Reuben squeezed my hand. 'He just needs to clear his head. He'll be back on track by the time we get back to the ludus, I bet you. Now, let's get to work.'

To my astonishment he calmly sat down in the dark. After a few seconds, rays of pure white light started streaming from his hands and heart. Apparently Reuben intended to spring clean the whole temple!

'OK, angel-boy, I get the message,' I sighed. 'But can we make it quick?'

But my buddy refused to budge, until we'd neutralised every speck of PODS contamination, and filled the space with uplifting vibes.

As we left, I caught a flicker of movement in the porch. I thought it was some old rags blowing in the wind, then I looked again and saw a beggar huddled in the shadows. You couldn't really tell how old he was. He was little more than skin and bone. But something in his eyes made me look twice.

'Excuse me,' I said. 'We're looking for a Vestal called Lucilla. You don't know what happened to her, do you?'

The beggar's voice was so quiet, I had to crouch down to hear him.

'They took her to the Field of Sorrows.'

I didn't like the sound of this. 'Where on earth is that?'

'It's where they take Vestals who offend the goddess. They're going to bury her alive,' the beggar said sombrely.

I gasped with horror. 'Just for letting the flame go out! But that wasn't even her fault!'

'Lucilla is charged with a second offence,' said the beggar in a low voice.

155

'A temple elder accused her of meeting a young man in secret.'

'But she didn't, right?' said Reuben.

'Lucilla has served the goddess faithfully since she was ten years old,' said the beggar. 'She would never do anything to dishonour her.'

'Can you tell us where to find this field?' Reuben asked.

The beggar gave us detailed directions.

'You've been really helpful.' I started fumbling in the purse at my waist and held out the usual small coins.

To my surprise, he waved them away. 'It was my pleasure to help you. Thank you for cleaning up in there, by the way. It didn't go unnoticed.'

I stared at him. This was not normal behaviour for Ancient Roman beggars. Plus there was something about his eyes. 'Omigosh!' I gasped. 'You're an—'

The Earth angel quickly put his fingers to his lips. 'When you see Orlando, tell him what happened here was not his fault,' he whispered urgently. 'But he has to hurry. He's

156

running out of time.'

I was still beside myself with embarrassment. 'You must think I'm so rude—I had NO idea!!'

The Earth angel gave a soft laugh. 'You weren't supposed to recognise me. We try to tread carefully in Dark eras. Most of us cloak our vibes to keep the Dark powers off the scent.'

'But not at the Games,' said Reuben.

'No, not at the Games.' I saw the angel's teeth flash in the shadows. 'We also give the occasional cosmic nudge!'

*   *   *

We found Orlando back at the gladiator school, battering the daylights out of a straw target in the dark.

'We know where they've taken Lucilla!' I panted out. 'Plus we've got a message for you.'

The Earth angel's message had a totally luminous effect. Orlando immediately threw off his depression and beamed telepathic signals to the rest of the task force. Dazed-looking angels emerged from their sleeping

157

quarters to join us under the stars.

'What's going on?' asked a confused trainee. 'Are we going home?'

'I wish,' someone sighed. 'I've had enough boiled barley to feed a Roman legion.'

'Barley's good for gladiators. It makes your blood clot,' said another trainee in a cheerful voice.

'It makes *everything* clot,' said the second trainee darkly.

Orlando waited until everyone had settled down, then he started to talk. He was one hundred percent back in leader mode; calm, collected, totally focused. First Orlando had to fill everyone in about Aurelia and her long lost sisters.

'The aim of this mission was to bring the three girls together,' he explained. 'But the Agency advised me not to make this generally known. They said there were cosmic spies on every street corner in Nero's Rome, monitoring conversations, even thoughts.' Orlando gave a rueful laugh. 'I thought this was paranoid to be honest. But it looks as if their caution was justified. A few hours

158

ago we went to make contact with the third triplet. Somehow—I've no idea how—the Opposition found out and got there first.'

I was glad it was dark so no-one could see me going red.

'That might have been my fault,' I mumbled.

Orlando looked startled. 'What do you mean?'

'I saw Lucilla coming out of the temple, when we were being taken to the dungeons. I was so stunned by her resemblance to Aurelia, I just blurted it out. One of our guards must be a spy for the PODS. I'm sorry, everyone,' I said humbly. 'That's the only way it could have happened.'

Reuben was twiddling one of his baby dreads. 'No way was this your fault, Mel. You had no idea then that Aurelia was one of triplets. And you definitely didn't know she and her sisters were caught up in a cosmic tug of war.'

'It IS my fault,' I said miserably. 'I'm a total motor mouth.'

'I agree with Reuben. You shouldn't

blame yourself,' said Orlando. 'But unless we get Lucilla back, this mission will be a write-off.'

'So let's get her!' called someone.

'This isn't going to be like sneaking prisoners past drunken guards,' Orlando told him. 'We'll have to fight.'

'Surely we aren't allowed to use angelic fighting skills on humans?' said a trainee in alarm.

Orlando's reply chilled me to the bone. 'The beings who took Lucilla from the temple aren't human.'

* * *

Just occasionally you find an Earth location that feels like it's twinned with a Hell dimension. The Field of Sorrows was one of those.

It was the dead of night when we rumbled up in Festus's wagon, but the air was so thick with human despair, you could practically taste it. We'd arrived just as the tail-end of a silent torchlight procession was disappearing in through the gates.

I could sense Orlando psyching

himself up. 'Once we're in there, there's only one way out—the hard way,' he said tensely. 'So put up your energy shields and keep them up. I don't want you guys contaminated with evil energy. I don't want any casualties tonight. Good luck everyone.'

We slipped through the gates and began to mingle with the crowd.

'What are all these people doing here?' I whispered nervously.

'It's a public ritual,' Orlando said. 'Anyone can come.'

After the Roman Games you'd think I'd be unshockable but the idea that humans would trek out to this desolate place in the dark, to gawk at a teenage girl being buried alive, left me speechless.

They weren't all sightseers. At the head of the procession, priests, senators and government officials walked ceremoniously behind a curtained litter. The sight made me shiver. Lucilla was by herself in there, waiting to go to her death, and these people were just going to stand and watch it happen.

The procession wound its way to higher ground. In the flickering torchlight, I noticed ominous mounds like giant mole-hills.

Reuben went wide-eyed. 'Is that where—?'

'I don't want to talk about it,' I said huskily. It was hard to talk in the Field of Sorrows actually. The terrible vibes made the words dry up in your mouth. The only sounds were the hypnotic tramp of people's sandalled feet over strangely hollow-sounding ground and the occasional phlegmy cough of one of the litter bearers.

This is a funeral march, I thought in horror. It was like Lucilla was officially dead already.

The flaring torches cast dramatic shadows on people's faces. Most of them had the sharp cheekbones of the chronically poor, yet their eyes glittered with excitement. Probably the temple scandal and Lucilla's gruesome punishment were the most thrilling events to have happened in ages.

At last the procession stopped beside a newly dug pit. When I saw the rungs of the crude wooden ladder protruding from the earth, I had to dig my nails into my palms. I couldn't believe these people were actually going through with this.

The bearers set down the litter at the edge of the pit. Two temple flunkeys drew back the curtains and lifted Lucilla out, bound and gagged and still dressed in her white tunic and gauzy bridal veil. I tried not to imagine how terrified Aurelia's sister must be.

It seemed the authorities couldn't just dump a dishonoured Vestal virgin in a hole and leave her there. First they had to blow horns and chant, and a priest had to say pompous words in Latin about how wicked and sinful she was.

The dreary ritual seemed to go on for ever, yet Lucilla stood perfectly motionless, with her bound hands clasped in front of her, looking completely serene. Even her thoughts were serene. I know this because I could hear them as clearly as if she'd spoken them aloud. *Mother goddess, you know I am innocent. Give me the courage to bear my fate.*

At the end of the ceremony, five women stepped forward, looking as if they were going to a bizarre Roman housewarming. Two were clutching dishes of food, a third carried a jug of wine and the fourth hugged a folded blanket in her arms. The fifth woman held a lighted lamp, and seemed to be having trouble sheltering the flame from the wind that blew over the open ground.

'They have to leave Lucilla enough provisions to last twenty-four hours,' Orlando whispered. 'Otherwise it's sacrilege.'

'But it's OK for her to be suffocated from lack of oxygen, is it?' I hissed angrily.

'No, of course it's not OK. But most of these people believe she insulted the goddess. To them that's like insulting Rome. They think she's a traitor to Rome. The way they see it, if they don't punish Lucilla, Vesta will withdraw her protection and the Roman Empire will fall.'

People were crowding closer to the

pit. I could feel their excitement rising. I broke into total goosebumps as I recognised the PODS who'd been at Quintus's nightmarish banquet.

Why are you surprised, Melanie? I thought in disgust. They framed this innocent girl to stop us reuniting her with her sisters. Naturally they'll be in at the kill.

For PODS this was like the ultimate cosmic joke. And as always, they'd manipulated gullible humans into doing their dirty work for them.

One of the flunkeys started to untie Lucilla's ankles. I felt myself go dizzy with horror. They were going to make Aurelia's sister climb down into her own grave!

Then Orlando's signal flashed through me like volts down a wire.

Go go go!!

In that confused nanosecond, before mixed-up Melanie Beeby turned into Helix, the heavenly whirlwind, I relived my fantasy: me and Orlando fighting bravely side by side. Well, now it was happening for real. And it *was*n't thrilling and it certainly *was*n't romantic, and it *totally* didn't matter how I looked. The world had narrowed down to a single urgent thought. Saving Lucilla.

I have a theory about what happened. I think these particular PODS had been sponging off Ancient Roman humans for too long. They'd got the impressive spy network, plus they could bump off inconvenient humans if they had to, and they thought that was enough. They'd lost their edge, basically. It just didn't occur to these creeps that a ragtag bunch of unarmed celestial trainees would charge out of the crowd and put a stop to their murderous plans! And as every warrior knows, surprise is the best weapon.

OK, so I might have squealed like a girl when my first Roman lookalike melted in front of my eyes, but then my angelic training kicked in and I focused like I've never focused before. Fighting PODS is unbelievably hideous. One minute I was kicking the sassafras out of something that looked like a human. Then, euw! I was grappling with a slimy monster from my darkest nightmares.

Plus, whenever I glanced up, I'd see my fellow angels doing battle with their own horrors.

But that wasn't the worst thing. The worst thing was having to get up close and personal to beings who are basically pure evil energy.

This full-on cosmic combat lasted ten minutes max from start to finish. For the *bona fide* humans in the crowd, it must have been a horrifying spectacle. Most of them fled in terror including, it has to be said, the priests. But one by one the PODS were beaten back, their human forms dissolving into the earth. The only signs they'd ever existed were these like, glistening trails of slime.

Reuben and I immediately started to untie Lucilla.

Orlando sounded so calm, you'd think we'd just completed a successful Dark Studies exercise back home. 'Excellent work, team. Now let's get out of here. We've won the battle, but that doesn't mean we've won the war. Next time they'll be ready for us.'

'Did the goddess send you?' Lucilla

167

asked us in awe.

'Just think of us as your friends,' grinned Reuben.

'And your sisters' friends,' I said impulsively.

Lucilla gasped. 'My sisters? But I don't—'

'It's a long story,' Reuben said. 'We'll tell you on the way.'

On the way back to the gate, Lucilla kept glancing back uneasily, and I heard her whisper a prayer to the goddess. She was remembering those terrible mounds, the graves of Vestals who were not so lucky.

I linked my arm through hers. 'Come on,' I said. 'This is the first day of the rest of your life.'

And we walked away from the Field of Sorrows.

CHAPTER ELEVEN

Lucilla said very little on our journey back. She mostly rested with her eyes closed. A few times I saw her snatch a shy peek around the crowded wagon. I think she needed to reassure herself that we were real, that she wasn't actually down a pit, just hallucinating being rescued. Once she said, 'What did you say their names were?'

I patted her hand. 'Star and Aurelia.'

'All our names are full of light,' she said softly.

'What does Aurelia mean?'

'The golden one.' Lucilla closed her eyes again.

'This has to be the longest night in history,' I said to Reuben. 'I feel like I've been charging about Ancient Rome forever.'

'Well it's nearly over now,' he said comfortingly.

I put my lips close to his ear. 'Am I the only person here who thinks this is a teeny bit scary?' I whispered. 'Orlando is defying a seriously evil curse. Remember all that stuff about cosmic black holes? Who knows what will happen when we put these triplets together?'

Reuben gave me one of his pure angel smiles. 'The Agency wants them reunited,' he said. 'So it'll all work out. Relax!'

We dropped the rest of the guys off at the barracks. Reuben, Orlando, Lucilla and I walked across the courtyard to Star's apartment.

To my dismay someone had broken several branches off the peach tree. The fallen fruit was trampled into mush.

Orlando turned pale. 'Festus told two men to watch the door. Where are they?'

Oh no, I thought. Please please no!

The door was open. Inside Juno was trying to comfort a sobbing Aurelia. Festus Brutus hovered unhappily.

'Where's Star?' Orlando said at once.

'Nero sent for her,' he growled.

'At this hour?' I said.

'Couldn't sleep apparently,' said Festus in disgust. 'His advisers thought a private performance from Rome's most famous gladiatrix would while away the night. I tried to stop them lad, but I'm not the man I was.'

I could tell the old gladiator felt

ashamed that he wasn't able to protect his protégée.

'You've been a good friend to Star,' said Orlando. 'You mustn't reproach yourself.'

Aurelia was still sobbing with her hands over her face. She'd got to the stage where you can hardly breathe. Lucilla went to kneel beside her. She gazed at this unknown sister in awe, as if she was afraid she would vanish. With a trembling hand, she reached out to stroke her hair. 'My sister,' she said softly. 'The goddess showed you to me in visions, but I never thought we would meet in this world.'

Aurelia's face was red and swollen from crying. She peered at Lucilla incredulously. 'You're the temple girl! Mella found you!'

'Not just me,' I said awkwardly.

'Oh, this is so strange! I just found and lost one sister. Now you—' Aurelia broke off and gave a slightly hysterical laugh. 'I can't take it in. I feel deranged. I don't know if I should tremble, weep, or jump about with happiness!'

Lucilla sat beside Aurelia and took her hand. Her eyes sparkled with tears. 'We should be happy,' she said softly. 'A Dark power forced us to travel this life alone. Now the gods have brought us back together and we can fulfil our destiny.'

Woo! I thought. This triplet was totally luminous! She practically had her own personal hotline to the gods. She knew exactly what was going on!!

Unfortunately we still only had two triplets in our possession.

'The PODS really shoved a spanner in the works this time.' I sighed to Orlando.

But now they'd taken Star, he was like this unstoppable force. 'They slowed us down a bit, that's all,' he said. 'We know Star is at Nero's palace. We'll reunite them there.'

Personally, I would not have chosen an imperial palace full of PODS, plus their human sympathisers, for the triplets' reunion, but I suspected there was a crucial element of cosmic timing, which Orlando was keeping to himself; so for once I decided not to argue.

172

*   *   *

Nero's palace was in the super deluxe area of Rome, high on a leafy hill, well away from the noise and smells of the common people. It wasn't too hard to sneak into the palace grounds. No CCTV cameras or electric gates in those days.

The trouble started when we tried to get in through the kitchens. We'd forgotten that all Nero's slaves were dressed in identical livery, to show they belonged to the imperial household. A slave sussed us the instant we put our noses inside.

'What's this? The cabaret?' he said sarcastically.

The cheeky answer just jumped out of my mouth. 'Yeah, we're the dancing girls, and these are our body guards.'

I heard Orlando making choking sounds.

The slave grinned. 'Then you won't mind letting me see you dance.'

'No problem,' I said confidently. Well, raunchy dancing is universal,

173

right? I showed him a few sexy dance moves.

He shook his head. 'All young girls can dance. So if you're the cabaret, where are your costumes?'

'Oh, duh,' I said. 'Like we could walk through the streets in those without being arrested. We sent them over earlier. With, erm, the musicians,' I improvised hastily.

The slave laughed. 'Nice try, darling. Now get out before someone from Security sees you and things get nasty.'

But I had no intention of leaving. This was absolutely the only way I knew to reach Star. 'Look, ask the Emperor, if you don't believe me!' I said desperately.

The slave shook his head in mock despair. 'There's no helping some people.' He bellowed into the distance. 'Guards!'

Orlando and Reuben were looking at me as if I'd lost my mind.

'I know what I'm doing; OK?' I hissed. 'You want to get the sisters back together don't you? What does it matter if we're taken before Nero as prisoners or, like, his naughty hoochy-coochy dancers?'

A look of grudging respect came into Orlando's eyes. 'Melanie Beeby,' he murmured, 'you are something else.'

Nero's household guards marched us down gleaming corridors, through a pair of gigantic doors, and into a marble dining hall filled with loud drunken voices and the busy clattering of cutlery. The smell of complicated Roman sauces floated through the air. The Emperor had insomnia, so naturally he was giving a nocturnal feast for all his pervy friends and relations.

A group of musicians were playing valiantly at one end of the hall. You could hardly hear the instruments through the gales of talk and laughter.

Nero himself reclined on a golden couch, among gold tasselled cushions, wearing a white silk toga, with a gold striped border. The Emperor's laurel wreath had slipped down over one eye, and he was smacking his lips over a plate of little roasted birds. I tried not to look too closely, but judging from their size they were blackbirds or thrushes.

On the other side of a low table, Titus Lucretius was tossing raw oysters into that wet-looking red mouth of his. Beside him Quintus steadily knocked back the booze.

The guard cleared his throat. 'Your majesty, these children were discovered sneaking into the palace. They claim to be a troupe of barbarian dancers, majesty.'

Nero's midnight party had put him in a mellow mood. 'But these are the lion children,' he said in a mild voice. I saw his eyelids droop briefly as he registered the extraordinary resemblance between Aurelia and her sister. 'My, my,' he crooned. 'One Christian and one Vestal virgin. How enchanting. You came at the right moment,' he told them confidingly. 'Just in time for the evening's main attraction.'

'With respect,' Titus interrupted smoothly, 'your majesty does remember that these are intruders, not invited guests?'

Nero's face darkened. 'Which of us

is the *Emperor?*' he demanded.

'You, of course, your majesty, but—'

'Then I think I can decide who to invite into my own palace, Titus Lucretius,' said the Emperor haughtily. He jumped up and his plate of little dead birds fell to the floor with a crash. Broken pottery and gravy went everywhere.

'Let me show you my surprise!' he told Aurelia and Lucilla in a conspiratorial voice. Seizing their hands he pulled them over to another set of doors. A slave hastily flung them open.

'Behold!' said Nero proudly.

There's something about madness that makes you feel crazy yourself. And when I saw what was on the other side of the doors, I literally felt dizzy, as if reality was turning inside out.

Nero had built an amphitheatre inside his palace. It was on a smaller scale, but apart from that everything was identical; the tiers of seats, the sand-filled arena. As it was night-time, the arena wasn't flooded with Mediterranean sunlight, but lit by

177

burning torches.

The Emperor's guests filed in to take their seats. Some brought their full plates and goblets with them, and carried on gorging themselves and gossiping loudly. The Emperor made us sit with him in the front row. As his new special best friends, Aurelia and Lucilla had to sit on either side of him.

'They brought a little gladiatrix here for my amusement,' Nero drawled. 'But ordinary armed combat is so boring. So I decided to introduce an element of surprise.' He clapped his hands. 'Bring her in!'

When I saw Star led into the arena by the guards, I practically bit through my lip to stop myself crying out. She'd come to fight, yet they'd taken away her sword, her shield and all her protective armour. In her white linen tunic she looked desperately small and vulnerable.

But when Nero set eyes on her, he looked totally stunned. His eyes swivelled nervously to Lucilla and Aurelia, then returned to the gladiatrix.

Omigosh! I thought. It's the first

time he's seen her without her mask! Beads of perspiration appeared on the Emperor's forehead and he began to breathe in panicky gasps. I felt almost sorry for him. Hanging out with PODS was doing absolutely nothing to improve Nero's mental health.

'It's OK, your majesty,' I said in my most gentle voice. 'You're not imagining things. The girls are identical triplets. This is the first time they've been together since they were ba—'

'Silence, foolish girl!' barked Nero. He hastily blotted his sweaty face with the silken hem of his toga. 'Obviously I realised they're triplets!' he hissed at me. 'Do you think I'm insane?'

Oops, I thought.

The PODS in the audience looked visibly disturbed when they saw Star separated from her sisters by just a flimsy wooden barrier and a few metres of sand. This was something they definitely hadn't bargained for. And then two concealed gates burst open, and ten fully-armed gladiators stormed in.

This was the Emperor's surprise element. Nero wanted to see the gladiatrix fight for her life against impossible odds, and finally expire in a pool of blood. So did all his sick cronies. The amphitheatre erupted into hyena-type whoops of excitement.

But when Star saw what entertainment Nero had laid on for his guests, she did something extraordinary. The girl who'd had to fight to survive for practically her whole life, silently knelt down in front of the Emperor, bowed her head, and totally refused to fight.

Nero was beside himself. 'Get up, get up!' he screamed.

Star didn't move.

The gladiators came to a stumbling halt. They were the kind of guys you'd hate to meet in a dark alley: scary professional killers, skilled in every fighting style going, and proud of it. But murdering a kneeling girl requires no skill whatsoever. They stared at Star like puzzled bulldogs.

The sweethearts, I thought deliriously. They totally can't do it!

But the mad Emperor wasn't going to be cheated now. A creepy smile spread over his face. 'Guards!' he bellowed. 'I'm introducing one last challenge for the gladiatrix.'

He jerked Lucilla and Aurelia to their feet. 'Take them into the arena to join their sister!' he announced.

CHAPTER TWELVE

Aurelia gave me a beseeching look as she and Lucilla were led away.

I could feel the air seething with dark vibes. The PODS were seriously alarmed. No way did they want these sisters in Nero's arena. But the Emperor had spoken and he had to be obeyed.

Orlando had gone totally white, and Reuben was frantically twiddling one of his dreads. This was so not how any of us had pictured this reunion.

Like Brice said, the Emperor was seriously psycho. He was determined to force Star to perform, and he'd come up with the perfect scenario. The gladiatrix could never stand by and watch as her sisters were slaughtered. She'd rather die defending them.

For the first time since they were babies, the triplets were only metres apart. For a moment no one moved, and then in one supple movement Star rose to her feet and she did this really touching thing. She walked right up to her long lost sisters and looked wonderingly into their eyes, the way a trusting small child would do, and her sisters gazed wonderingly back at her.

I thought my heart was going to burst. 'That's SO sweet,' I whispered.

'They're remembering each other's vibes,' Reuben said softly.

Star briefly closed her eyes. I saw tears spill down her face. Aurelia and Lucilla spontaneously reached for their sister's hands and as the three girls touched, a shiver of cosmic electricity went through me.

Orlando sighed with pure relief. We'd done it.

The amphitheatre was in total confusion. Some gladiators charged at the triplets, then thought better of it. Others just gave helpless shrugs and let their swords fall to the ground. The audience was outraged. They started stamping and chanting, 'Kill! Kill Kill!'

The girls were oblivious to all of this. Their rapture at finding each other had enclosed them in a kind of joyous force-field. To them, nothing else existed. The mad Emperor, this toy arena and the audience of baying upper-class Romans, was a meaningless illusion. Only their love was real.

When human love is that pure, it can move mountains. It can stop the murderous onslaught of trained gladiators. It can send such beautiful, electrifying shock waves through the air, that an evil dynasty finally begins to crumble.

I became aware of disturbing grinding sounds far beneath the earth, as if the tectonic plates or whatever, were shifting. Hairline cracks appeared in the palace walls and a marble statue of the Emperor wobbled unsteadily on its plinth. None of this cosmic upheaval registered with the humans. Not yet. It was more like an angelic trailer of things to come.

Omigosh! I thought. Is this what happens when you reverse a hideous Ancient Roman curse?

I glanced at Orlando for reassurance, but he was watching the reunited sisters with a dreamy expression. His mission had worked out just like it was supposed to. Against all the odds, we'd succeeded in getting these three extraordinary sisters into the same space, and let me tell you, their combined energy was awesome. I could literally feel it pulsing through me like light from a star.

Aah, I thought blissfully. This is just the best job in the universe.

That's one major difference between us and the Dark agents. PODS operatives are never moved by human emotions. And by this stage in his career, Titus Lucretius was three-quarters of the way to being a POD. I vaguely registered him edging stealthily towards the barrier, but I didn't see him reach inside his toga.

My angel buddy did. Frantic thoughts flew from his mind to mine. *He's got a dagger! He's going to* kill Aurelia!

Vaulting over anyone in his way, Reuben launched himself wildly at Titus. In my desperation to reach Aurelia, I hurled myself over the barrier into the arena and fell heavily on my knees, taking off a layer of skin.

Star was faster than any of us. She saw the dagger flash towards her sister and simply stepped in front of her to block the blow.

I wanted to scream at the top of my lungs, but somehow all my pain and shock stayed trapped inside.

Titus's dagger had pierced Star through the heart. It looked all wrong sticking out of her body. Stupid, grotesque and wrong. A crimson flower of blood came welling up around the hilt of the dagger, soaking through the white linen of her tunic.

The gladiatrix quickly pressed her hand to the wound and tried to smile. 'I thought it would be today,' she managed to say. 'I told Juno I would die today. Don't look so sad,' she told her horrified sisters softly. 'I'll be waiting for you in the Elysian fields.' Then she crumpled in sickening slow motion.

Lucilla and Aurelia tried to catch her, but Star sagged emptily in their arms and all three of them ended up sprawling on the ground.

There was a silence so total, that it was more shattering than any sound. I felt as if I'd been murdered too. I couldn't believe this vibrant beautiful girl was dead. Then just as I thought my head would explode with horror, the scene became oddly fixed and silent.

It was like in *Sleeping Beauty,* when people all over the castle get frozen in really dumb positions. Romans, wearing laurel wreaths and clutching lumps of roast chicken, craned forward to get a good view of the dead gladiatrix.

Titus was exchanging a frozen grin of triumph with Aurelia's brother. A horrified gladiator continued to stare down helplessly at the stricken girls cradling their dead sister.

Was this some bizarre side-effect of the curse? I wondered. And if so, why weren't we frozen too? I could hear Reuben breathing unevenly. Plus I could feel my own heart hammering behind my ribs.

Someone else was moving too, making his way slowly and shakily past these bizarre human waxworks and into the arena.

Orlando looked like someone who'd got trapped inside a bad dream and couldn't wake up. He knelt beside Star and his face was grey with shock. 'Why couldn't I save you? I should have saved you,' he whispered.

My throat ached so much I could hardly speak. 'You couldn't know,' I told him painfully. 'They were so happy. It just didn't seem possible anything bad could happen.'

Reuben was looking around him nervously. His sharper angelic senses had picked something up.

'What's happening?' I asked in alarm.

I felt a powerful disturbance in the

air, like the beating of invisible wings. A shaft of light came down and Michael appeared beside us. Wouldn't you know it, I thought bitterly, now it's too late, the Agency's stepped in.

I wanted to throw myself into Michael's arms and beg him to take me home. I wanted to kick and scream like a bratty little girl. 'Why did you let it happen? Why did you let Star die?!'

But my inner angel refused to let me give in to these immature impulses. She just watched and waited to see what would happen next.

In his despair, Orlando didn't seem to register Michael's arrival.

When he didn't look up, Michael touched him very lightly between the shoulder blades. The whoosh of cosmic energy seemed to jolt Orlando out of his trance. 'They were together for less than three minutes,' Orlando's voice was flat with misery. 'And now she's dead. I didn't even see it coming.'

'There was nothing you could have done,' Michael said softly. 'I know how it seems, but everything is completely as it should be. Now we have to get these two girls to safety.'

Michael bent over Lucilla and Aurelia. I saw a flicker of light go through them. If I had been them I'd have wanted to stay frozen forever. When the surviving two sisters saw Star still lying dead in their arms, their faces were pitiful.

'I have to take her now,' Michael told them.

I heard Aurelia gasp and their eyes filled with awe. I wondered what the sisters were seeing. Could they see Michael's crumpled suit and his beautiful archangel eyes? Or did they see some anonymous figure with wings?

Michael lifted Star's lifeless body in his arms. A pearly haze of white light began to form. It softly enfolded the sisters, growing brighter and more intense until they were completely hidden from view.

Once again I felt that odd thrumming disturbance as Time switched back on. But by this time Michael and the girls were nowhere to be seen.

189

There was major pandemonium as the amphitheatre returned to life. Obviously the humans didn't suss that an angel had spirited the sisters through a gap in time. But they knew they'd witnessed some kind of supernatural event.

Nero became totally unhinged and started screaming at the guards. 'It's sorcery! Taming lions! Vanishing triplets! I won't allow it! Search the palace from top to bottom!'

Guards came running. Gee thanks, Michael, I thought nervously. How do we get out of this?

'Go through every box room and latrine until you find those two sorceresses,' Nero was ranting. 'And those other prisoners!' he added vaguely.

Other prisoners? I glanced down at myself in confusion. Could he possibly mean us?

Orlando gave me a wan smile. 'Relax. We dematerialised a few moments ago.'

Reuben sagged with relief. 'Then let's get out of this hellhole!'

But someone had stepped in front of us, deliberately blocking our exit. Even in our non-material forms Titus Lucretius could see us perfectly. 'I'll find them if I have to move Heaven and Earth!' he hissed. 'Make no mistake, those sisters will die and their blood-line will die with them.'

'Time for a reality check, Titus,' Orlando said quietly. 'Haven't you noticed? You and your masters lost this one.'

Titus turned purple. 'Haven't YOU noticed?' he raged. 'I killed the gladiatrix, fool! The sisters have been separated for ever. WE defeated YOU!!'

Orlando shook his head. 'You're still part-human, though not for much longer at the speed you're mutating,' he added drily. 'So you don't understand that Time essentially has no meaning.'

'Oh please!' groaned Titus. 'Spare me the angelic hogwash!'

Orlando smiled. A real full-on smile. I could still see the shock and sadness in his eyes, but our boy was back.

'You really should get your evil masters to educate you,' he said calmly. 'From your limited human point of view the sisters' reunion was so brief as to be meaningless. But from a cosmic perspective, this event will resonate through human history until the end of Time itself.'

Titus stared at him open-mouthed.

'I'll explain,' said Reuben in a friendly voice. 'What Orlando means is that Star might be dead, but she still changed the world. Love is cool like that!'

'Come on,' said Orlando. 'Let's go home.'

*   *   *

Three days after we returned from our Roman mission, I scored a professional first and ended up in the hospital.

I was suffering from a massive overdose of PODS toxins, but I didn't know that, so after a hot shower and a change of clothes, I just went straight back to school. That's what you do when you're a professional. In my

192

opinion I was the same as normal, better actually.

OK, so it was harder to sleep at night since I came home, and when I finally managed to drop off, my dreams were v. disturbing. And OK, so for some reason it felt as if there was a sheet of frosted glass between me and my mates. But that didn't mean anything was wrong with me.

The bad nights meant I persistently slept through my alarm. Three mornings in a row, Lola went jogging on her own.

'Why didn't you wake me?' I complained when I caught up with her after morning school.

'I figured you needed the rest, Boo,' she said.

I gave her my brightest smile. 'I need to wake up my dozy angelic metabolism, that's all. Let's grab a salad, then we can at least go and work out in the gym.'

'Babe, don't take this the wrong way, but I think your tank is running on empty,' Lola said in an anxious voice. 'No, actually I think you're running on pure fumes. You should slow down. Give your energy system a chance to recover. You guys went through a lot.'

'Hey, there's nothing wrong with me,' I told her huffily. 'If you don't want to come that's fine. I'll go by myself!'

And that's what I did.

I was doing all right, until I went on the treadmill. There's something v. hypnotic about running on a never-ending conveyor belt. Maybe that's why I started having Ancient Roman flashbacks. Strangely, most of them were flashbacks to experiences I hadn't registered at the time. Like I could hear the exact tune the musicians played for the dancing girls as our litter bearers carried me and Aurelia past a sleazy bar.

And I kept seeing all these unknown Roman faces. The sunken eyes of an exhausted slave, as he used his last ounce of strength to help fellow slaves winch a slab of marble into place. The animated expressions of teenage girls at the baths, as they argued about which of their fave charioteers was the best looking.

Then I'd see my own hands fastening pearl hairpins into Aurelia's hair, as I dressed her for that horrible banquet. I never said goodbye, I realised. Aurelia was my human and I really respected her and *I never even said goodbye.*

But the disturbing flashbacks still kept coming: bloody executions, Christians chanting, the rungs of a wooden ladder sticking out of a newly dug pit. They came faster and faster and they wouldn't stop. I totally couldn't take it. My heavenly surroundings began to whirl around me, then suddenly, like the fadeout at the end of a movie, everything went black.

When I came round, I was lying in a white bed, surrounded by gauzy white curtains. An angel in pastel-coloured scrubs was calmly checking my pulse.

'You'll be fine,' he told me. 'You just need to rest, but we'd like to keep an eye on you for a couple of days. Would you like me to leave the curtains open?'

I tried to nod.

Drawing back the curtains, he went back out into the garden.

Sunlight and air came streaming in through the stone pillars and I could hear birds singing. I lay back weakly on my pillows and felt a soft breeze blow over my face. For the first time since I came back, I could smell the heavenly air, with its scent that is almost, but not quite, like lilacs. For absolutely no reason, tears began to seep from under my eyelids.

I cried on and off all the rest of that day, as distressing Roman memories floated to the surface. When I started crying about Star, the angel came in from the garden, smelling of rain and flowers, and silently held my hand.

*   *   *

I slept all night without moving. I didn't even wrinkle the sheets.

I was woken by sunlight glinting in my eyelashes. When I opened my eyes, Lola was sitting by my bed, rosy-faced from her early morning run. I threw my arms around her. 'I missed you so much!'

My soul buddy freed herself apologetically. 'Me too, Boo. But I am also a *leetle* bit sweaty as you can probably tell! You might want to leave the hug till later.'

'Lollie, after Ancient Rome, angelic sweat smells like roses!' I giggled.

On the last night of my PODS detox, Michael dropped by to see how I was getting on. By this time I was ready to talk about things that still bothered me. The curse for instance.

'That curse said if the triplets came back together, Rome would fall,' I said earnestly. 'Well, we got them back together, Michael, and I literally felt Rome's foundations shaking. I don't know how it seems to you guys, but I got the definite impression that Nero was, erm, *toast.*'

'And you're worried you might have done some harm.'

I chewed at my lip. 'Well, yes,' I admitted.

Michael smiled. 'Melanie, you helped to turn an evil curse into a blessing. Have you any idea what a rare and wonderful event that is?'

'A blessing?' I said dubiously. 'Are you sure?'

'I'm one hundred percent sure!' Michael flipped open his cool little laptop and set it up where I could see the screen. 'You might want to take a look at these.'

He started to scroll through a huge picture gallery of human faces. To me it seemed like they came from every race, era, and civilisation. Male, female, black, white, golden and brown, the faces flowed on and on.

Now and then Michael would single one out, like: 'Of course if Marie hadn't shown such exceptional courage, radium would never have been invented.' Or: 'Rosa's refusal to be a second-class citizen, helped to give birth to the American civil rights movement.'

I was baffled. 'I don't get it. What have these people got in common?'

'I've been waiting for you to ask me that,' he beamed.

Michael tapped a key and made the portrait gallery disappear.

Now only two faces gazed out at me. I felt the slow dawning of recognition. They were older in these pictures, but the strength and beauty of Aurelia and Lucilla's faces shone through, totally unaltered.

'All those humans were descended from just two sisters?' I said in amazement.

'Every last one,' he said firmly.

'And they all did these incredible things?'

'They were all incredible people, which isn't quite the same thing. The kind of humans who change the atmosphere of the planet for the better, just by being themselves.'

Michael gave me an unusually mischievous smile. 'In fact if you yourself were to trace your human family tree all the way back to Roman times, you might get a surprise, Melanie!'

'Yeah, right,' I grinned. 'Which Ancient Roman triplet am I descended from?'

'Aurelia, obviously,' said Michael in the same light-hearted voice. 'There's a very strong connection between the two of you, which I think you noticed.'

This idea was way too fanciful for me. I was just happy to know that Aurelia and her sister survived to live happy productive lives. Plus it gave me a definite buzz to know we'd had a hand in such significant historical events, however indirectly.

Next morning, Lola came to take me home. 'I thought we'd drop into Guru on the way back,' she said. 'My treat.'

I felt a flicker of panic. 'I don't know if I'm ready to see people yet, Lollie.'

'Sorry Boo,' said my soul-mate in a firm voice. 'You won't be fully recovered until you've had Guru's infallible chocolate brownie cure.'

'Lola, that is SO low!' I giggled. 'You know I can't resist!'

It felt strange walking through the lively streets of the Ambrosia quarter, after the blissful peace of the sanctuary. When we eventually reached Guru, I saw a familiar figure slouched at an outdoor table.

Brice whipped off his shades and

gave me a cool stare. 'Hi, Melanie, how was Ancient Rome?'

'Excuse us,' I said politely. I dragged Lola into a huddle. 'I really appreciate you inviting me out,' I hissed, 'but I'm not playing cosmic gooseberry to you and lover boy. I'll wander back to school, OK? And you and Brice have a brownie for me.'

'Sit,' said Lola threateningly.

'Yeah, Melanie, sit,' said Brice. 'You might have to wait a while. The new waitress is still learning the ropes.'

It was unexpectedly nice sitting in the sun in my fave student hangout. I even found myself telling Brice about stuff. Stuff that to my surprise, he seemed to understand.

'What I don't get is what made them change,' I said. 'Like, we hear about major cosmic events shaking up Planet Earth's climate, thundering great meteorites, ice ages and whatever. But they never tell you what it takes to shake up human hearts. I mean how did humans get from the Field of Sorrows to, well—Greenpeace and Save the Children and whatever.'

201

'Evolution?' Brice suggested wickedly.

I put my hands over my ears. 'Aaargh! That word drives me nuts. No, it had to be a miracle. It's the only possible explanation.'

Brice gave me a funny grin and began whistling to himself. After a while I recognised the tune. It was *Sisters are Doing it for Themselves*.

I stared at him in bewilderment. What was it Reuben told Titus? That Star might be dead, but she'd still helped to save the world.

'Omigosh,' I breathed. 'The sisters did that? They changed the hearts of the whole world?'

'The sisters and their children and their children's children,' said Brice carelessly. 'You could call it a miracle. Or you could just call it evolution. Our order's taking a long time,' he called to Mo as he zipped past with a tray of smoothies.

'Sorry, our new girl is still finding her feet,' he explained. There was a loud crash from inside the café. Mo hastily excused himself.

'Uh-oh,' said Lola under her breath.

Orlando was standing by our table. 'I heard you'd been ill,' he said shyly. 'Are you OK now?'

'She loved the flowers you sent her,' said Brice mischievously.

'Shut up!' I hissed.

Orlando ignored him. 'You and Reuben really did great work.'

Lola gave him one of her looks. 'Boo's the best,' she said.

The new waitress came backing out through the door with her tray.

'Wait!' called Mo. 'You forgot the forks!'

Poor girl, she's really struggling, I thought.

Then I saw her face and the entire café went shimmery. It's no wonder I was shocked. The last time I'd seen her she'd had a knife through her heart, though it would have been really tasteless to mention it. Plus, in her new heavenly surroundings, Star's life as a gladiatrix seemed oddly irrelevant, like old clothes she'd totally outgrown.

She looked incredibly stylish actually, with her cool haircut, and her black and white waitressy outfit. The only reminder of her old life was the charm around her neck: a silver charm in the shape of a star.

'I'll see you when you get off work then,' Orlando told her softly.

Star glanced at him from under her lashes. 'Maybe,' she said in a considering kind of voice. 'If I'm not busy.'

To my surprise, it hardly hurt at all; though I couldn't explain this, even to myself. I still thought Orlando was the most beautiful boy in the universe, but after our Roman mission, I seemed to be seeing him in a less adoring light. Plus I liked Star. I liked her a lot. I wanted to get to know her better.

Wow, I've really changed, I thought.

Ahem, said my inner angel. You mean you've evolved.

Omigosh! I thought. It's true! Like, all this time, I'd been waiting for somebody (OK, Orlando!) to make me complete. But I didn't need Orlando, or any boy, to complete me. I had my fabulous mates, my totally luminous angel career, and best of all—I had ME!

Mel Beeby, feisty girl warrior, time-travelling stylist and celestial hip hop chick, was finally ready to move on!